# IN SUN

# DOWN FAR

## W. C. Highfield

Printed in the United States of America

ISBN  978-0-61511990-8

Library of Congress Control Number 2001119771

First Edition, Second Printing, 2010

To *Gayle*,
whose love, encouragement, and support
have made this possible

Set in Southwest Florida, IN SUN DOWN FAR chronicles events that take place during an eleven-day period in April 1990. The story concerns beach vendor Ellis Parkington's struggle to come to grips with his view of the complexities of human behavior. The music of the blues is interwoven throughout this tale of the ups and downs in friendships, relationships, and life on the tropical island of St. George Beach.

# Preface

Looking back on it now, if I had gotten more involved, things might have turned out better. Well, at least maybe differently. But hey, you can start to second-guess yourself if you go and stick your nose in other people's business. What the heck could I have done anyway? We're all adults. Sometimes that doesn't count for much. Especially when it comes to Harry. Yeah, Harry Forte, probably the biggest know-it-all in the history of the civilized world. Why did it have to be him to get the whole damn thing started? Well, it was already started. He just discovered it and then I didn't want to believe him. Geez, Harry claims to have the answer for everything. No wonder people don't want to believe him.

So here I sit, Ellis Parkington, age thirty-six, beach vendor extraordinaire. Purveyor of some of the unhealthiest foodstuffs that Southwest Florida's Gulf Coast has ever seen. And I can't sell enough of the junk. Don't people know they're poisoning them-selves? I mean, between the hot dogs loaded with all the fat and preservatives, the sodas with the sugar, or diet ones that have God knows what in them, it's truly amazing. My plan is to keep selling the crap for as long as the public wants to buy it. It's what I do. It's how I make a living, like they say.

I do enjoy dealing with the older folks, though. They roll right in at 10:00 a.m. when I open.

They've had their walk on the beach and the blood is really flowing through the old veins. Coffee and a bagel and they're feeling pretty sporty. They're something.

Anyway, I can't help it, but I keep thinking about everything that's happened lately. It's turned out that I'm happier about myself, but I do have this awful blend of anger and frustration all churning around inside of me. That's unusual, since I don't normally worry about much of anything. At least I haven't for the past sixteen years. That's when I moved here to St. George Beach. It seems like a lifetime ago now...

# 1

My grandparents moved to St. George Beach when I was a kid. They bought this little two-bedroom bungalow a couple of blocks off the beach. It was the typical "seniors retiring to Florida" deal. My parents and my older brother Walter and I would come down to visit every year at Easter and for a week in the summer. St. George Beach was a lot less crowded back then. I loved it. But what's not to love when you're a kid on vacation where it is warm and there's a beach? There were only a few motels on the island in those days and my father insisted the family stay in one while we were there. Not me. I would stay with Nana and Poppy and sleep in their second bedroom. Of course, they would always spoil me. Man, it was great.

My grandfather died when I was in high school and that was really rough on Nana. They had always done everything together, but Poppy had taken care of the finances. He was a detail guy. Nana felt kind of lost when it came to that sort of stuff. My father tried talking her into moving back up north to our house in Pennsylvania, but she didn't want any part of it. Over the years, she and Poppy had developed close friendships on the island. Nana really loved it there. She was staying. My dad spent a couple of weeks with her after my grandfather's funeral to help her adjust to her new life. I even stayed with her the entire summer between my junior and senior year. We got along fine. I took a job working as a beach vendor pushing one of those little carts. You learn a lot about handling cash doing that kind of work, and it stays with you. During that summer, Nana really got me into the healthy diet kick. Each day she'd load up a little cooler for me with fruit and raw vegetables and fish sandwiches. She didn't want me eating the junk I was selling to everybody on the beach. She had it right. My father always referred to me as a "health nut" after that summer. Heck, if you're going to be a nut about something, I'd say health is as good as it gets.

The following spring I graduated from West Chester High School, Class of 1972. It was automatic what was next. My father was a pharmacist and my brother was going to be a senior at Philadelphia College of Pharmacy. Take a stab in the dark at what I was going to do. It was one of those involuntary things. Like you didn't even have to think about it. My father was a pharmacist, my brother was going to be a pharmacist, and that's what was expected of me. It had been taken for granted for so long that it didn't require any thought. I think the brainwashing had been so complete I had convinced myself it was what I wanted to do. I'd always been pretty good at coming through with the things my parents and teachers expected of me. Personal desires and initiatives weren't part of the program in our family.

I made it through my freshman year in college without any major problems. I had a good study ethic and really kept my nose in the books. At that point, it was so far, so good. Early in my sophomore year, I met Claire. Well, I gotta tell you, I flipped. I mean, I'd had some girlfriends in high school, but they were nothing like this. Claire was planning to get into sales with a pharmaceutical company after she graduated. She was sharp as a tack, as in looks and brains. Man, I was nuts about her. Guess what? The day we get back to school from Christmas break, Claire tells me she's pregnant. I felt like somebody had hit me in the guts with a meat cleaver. By the way, that feeling didn't go away in an hour or two. I'm talking day and night. The first week after I found out I lost something like fifteen pounds. Weighing in at a hundred and fifty, it was a big drop. I couldn't eat or sleep.

To me, this predestination thing that had been going on my whole life, this paint-by-numbers format of my future, seemed shot to hell in a big way. I was crazy about Claire, but all of a sudden this seemed like a completely different subject. Apples and oranges. I would have traded the situation we were in with never having met her. In a heartbeat. I'm sorry, but that's just the way I felt. I had been funneled through this preplanned rat maze my whole life and now I'd really screwed it up. The shit had hit the fan and I was having tons of trouble not showing it.

Claire was pretty shook up, too, but it was different with her. I guess she thought I'd bite the bullet and "do the right thing." She made it seem like we could keep going on and work it out. That everything would be okay. We argued about it for a couple of weeks. When she finally faced up to my reluctance, which was less than thinly veiled, she was crushed. It had become very clear that I had no desire to be a twenty-year-old father. I tried to convince her it wasn't a good idea for either of us. Once she realized how strongly I felt about ending the pregnancy, our relationship became a house of cards. It was like a valve had been turned off on the pipeline through which our feelings for each other ran. Before too many weeks went by she had an abortion. Over and done. Neither of us ever told our parents. The last time I saw Claire was the day we walked out of the clinic. We were through. I can easily say those were the most awful three weeks of my life.

The whole thing took its toll on school. I didn't open a book for the first month of the second semester. Everything was a jumble to me. Even though the crisis was over, I was changed. I didn't care anymore. I didn't give a crap about anything. I was soured on what my life was about. It seemed so strange that it took that experience to make me begin to look at everything differently. What's important? What's happiness? What's peace of mind? What's there to value? I'd been playing the game my parents had set up for me all along. I had been plugged into their socket and had been running on their electric current. I stepped back and looked at my life and realized I wasn't happy.

So, in mid-February 1974, I dropped out of school. I wrote this long-ass letter explaining my feelings to my parents. I told them I couldn't go on with the college thing, the pharmacist thing. I figured it was a way I could put everything before them all at once without them picking my points apart piece by piece. Lay it all out. At least there would be no immediate rebuttal. In conversation, my parents were really good at interrupting if they didn't agree with me on any subject. The day after they read the letter, we had a meeting. Very formal. They were much calmer than I had expected. I got the impression they thought this was just a temporary phase I was going through. That I'd come to my senses in time. They were wrong. Maybe the way things were in the country at that time contributed to the way I felt. Maybe the way the Vietnam War had gone, the questioning of authority, or the rebellious spirit of young people had affected me. Maybe not. All I knew was I was through with school. I was through with close relationships with women. I was through with the whole ambition thing. I was consumed.

Although I never considered suicide, I had a boiling urge to get away from everything. To put together a plan to make the pain end. I knew where I could go. I called my grandmother and told her I wanted to come down and stay with her. She couldn't have been happier. On March 1, 1974 I loaded up my Opel station wagon and headed south for St. George Beach, Florida. When I arrived, Nana greeted me with open arms. She didn't question what I was doing. She wasn't disapproving of the change I was making in my life. From her standpoint, she was just plain happy I was there with her. I was happy, too. My parents called in those early days and occasionally wrote letters to make their plea for me to come home and go back to college. My stance about what I was doing was so strong that they became frustrated with me. The bond between us loosened and there became a distance between us greater than the actual miles we lived apart.

It didn't take long for me to figure out I had to do something to earn some money. Nana was comfortable with what she received from my grandfather's pension, but I wasn't staying with her just to freeload. I hooked up with the beach vendor I worked for the summer during high school when I had lived on the island. I started working for him again, hustling one of those little bicycle-operated carts up and down the beach. After a few months, my grandmother lent me enough money to buy my own vendor cart. I began slowly repaying her, but she made it clear that the debt wasn't a huge priority from her standpoint. Having me around meant more to her.

The cart was a larger and more stable kind, and it held a tremendous amount of provisions. I hauled it with my Opel wagon and stored it at night in Nana's garage. I got the proper license I needed and rented a spot at a popular beach access. The darn cart was so big I could even sit inside of it to conduct business, but that usually gave me a mild case of claustrophobia. I preferred to sit beside it in a director's chair, protected from the sun by a black-and-white-striped awning, which retracted into a roll on the top of the cart. In the mid-seventies, St. George Beach had not yet been commercialized to death. I was taking advantage of the sparseness of the place while I was getting my little operation set up. For St. George Beach it was the calm before the storm.

The first couple of years went by smoothly. Most of the time, I was pretty much of a homebody. Oh, I made friends. I'd spend time at the local watering hole, the Blue Moon, but inside I still felt shellshocked about my past. Nana was my companion and her house was my oasis. I'd get up early each morning and go over to the beach and swim in the Gulf of Mexico for a half hour or so. It wasn't like the ocean back up north. No waves. Just a gentle lapping of water onto the beach. The water was so clear, it could be up to your chest and you could still see your feet on the bottom. Sometimes I ran on the beach, but I liked swimming better. More peaceful. I'd heard swimming be compared to being back in the womb.

In time, my grandmother's health began to go downhill. Her heart was failing and there was a four or five month period when she was in and out of the hospital. The one thing Nana insisted on was she wouldn't go into a nursing home. She didn't want to be a burden to me, but she felt strongly about retaining her independence. Even though she was strong-willed, I kept a sharp eye on her. As her condition deteriorated, I'd close the cart up several times during the day to check on her, or I wouldn't open at all. Nana died in February 1978. In her will she left me her house and a modest savings. At her funeral, my parents remained as aloof and cool toward me as they had during the years I had lived with Nana. Nobody had much to say.

I adjusted to living alone. I continued to operate my vendor cart daily from ten until four. Some days after work I would go up to the Blue Moon. Other times I'd ride my bike, with my fishing gear on board, down to the south end of the island and try to catch dinner off of the bridge over Gateway Pass. It's a beautiful sight from that bridge. Looking to the west the inlet opens up into the magnificent Gulf of Mexico. Off the other side is a great view of Calusa Bay. Its water is a mix of greens and blues dotted with a series of mangrove islands. Because the Bay and the surrounding area is a preserve, the panorama in that direction probably hasn't changed in hundreds of years. I'd spend hours on that bridge. I loved it.

I had finally gained direct control of my life. When I wasn't working the cart, I did what I felt like and mixed with people on my own terms. I tried to never let myself be on anybody else's schedule. I made my own plans and changed them when I wanted. I truly believed I had found peace of mind, and the years rolled by...

....which brings us to last month, April 1990. It had been a busy "season" like we call it around here. The snowbirds were slowly filtering back up north and we were all done with the spring breakers. I'll tell you, I'd sold more junk out of my cart than any season I could remember. Every year there's more people, more construction, and more traffic. Not sure where or when it's going to end. The island can only support so much tonnage. We may end up sinking right into the Gulf someday. You don't hear any of the business types complaining though. They don't seem to give a damn about the overcrowding or any negative impact to the environment. More people and more buildings mean more money. Ah, the almighty dollar. I bet the Indians who lived here hundreds of years ago didn't think about things that way. I guess this is progress.

It was Wednesday and I closed up for the day. I went home, put the vendor cart away in the garage, and got my bike out. As I locked the garage door, I thought about Nana and Poppy and their connection to the house. I never forgot it was theirs before me, and I was proud of that heritage. I imagined they were probably up there in the clouds feeling happy that I continued to own the house. After all, I was carrying on the legacy of the property.

I grabbed a bottle of spring water and rode up the boulevard to the Blue Moon. Even though it was late in the afternoon, my trusty old plantation owner's hat was shielding the sun from my head and the back of my neck. If there's one thing I've learned here during these sixteen years, you've got to protect the skin. I know too many people who have fried themselves right into the doctor's office. It's nasty business if you're not careful.

When I got to the Blue Moon, I locked my bike to the rusted bicycle rack along the side of the building. The Blue Moon is a concrete block building that sits right on the beach. It was built back in the early fifties. I think the original owners wanted the place to be left standing if a hurricane ever made a direct hit. On the front wall is a mural of a tropical beach scene with a royal blue moon above. I glanced out over the Gulf and saw the sun's reflection shimmering brightly on the small peaks in the water as they lapped up on the beach. Noticing Harry Forte's pickup truck in the parking lot, I walked up the four brick steps and went inside. The double glass doors were propped open as usual. They would be closed during the summer months, however, because the outside heat made air-conditioning a requirement. Tom Grissom, who'd been the bartender for about ten years, caught my eye and was shaking his head while he pointed his thumb toward Harry Forte. Apparently, Harry had more than half a load on.

"What's up, Tommy?" I said.

"Nothing much, Ellis," said Tom. "Just another beautiful day in paradise and I'm stuck in here looking after the inmates."

"Hey, El, whatcha doin'?" slurred Harry.

"Hold on for a little bit there, Harry," I said. "I need to have a few beers before I'll be able to understand what you're saying."

"Very funny, Ellis," said Harry, raising the back of his hand and feigning a slap in my direction.

Tom came over and placed a cold draft on the bar in front of me and said, "I was hoping somebody would show up that I could turn Harry over to. The flag is up over his head."

"No problem, Tommy," I said. "I'm only having a couple and then I'll drive him home." Then I continued to Harry, "How about having a glass of water, my friend, and just relax and enjoy the view for a while."

"What?" said Harry, "I'm in the good ol' U.S. of A. I know my rights. I've read the Manual Charta."

"Manual Charta?" came a voice from across the bar. It was Roger Carson, a retired charter boat captain. He's an old salt if there ever was one. "It's Magna Charta, dufus. You know something, Harry? All the time you know every goddamn thing, and then you don't know a damn thing."

"Yeah, right," said Harry.

"I think you ought to take Ellis' advice, Harry," said Tom, the bartender. "Otherwise I'll have to ask you to move along."

"Harry, just sit here and check out that scene," I said, gesturing toward the large open double windows, which looked over the beach to the Gulf, "You won't find a better one."

"Oh, I've seen better," said Harry. "When I was in Hawaii I saw some views that would put this one to shame. And the time I—"

"Okay, okay," I interrupted. "Just take it easy and drink some water."

"Water over here, barkeep," called Harry, "but I guarantee you it won't taste as good as the rum I was drinking." While Harry's head was turned,

I grabbed his keys off the bar and put them in my pocket. I figured it was easier getting hold of them while he wasn't looking instead of playing tug of war later. Harry's a big guy.

"At your service M'Lord," said Tom, grabbing a plastic bottle of spring water from the cooler and putting it in front of Harry.

With the windows open toward the beach, and the front doors propped, an almost constant breeze flows through the Blue Moon. Even though it was sunny outside, large awnings over all of the windows kept the bar dark and comfortable. Entering in the daytime, it takes your eyes a few seconds to adjust to the sharp change in light. From the ceiling hang colorful Christmas lights, which stay up all year. The bar is u-shaped, with the open end leading to the kitchen on the right. The bill o' fare offered at the Blue Moon is limited to sandwiches and munchies. For what they serve, the quality of the food is consistently good. But it's one of those places where you don't want to see the kitchen or anybody who is working in it. To the left of the bar is a small stage where bands play several weeknights and on weekends. In general, the talent level of the bands that played at the Blue Moon was mediocre. Most of the groups came from the city of St. George, which is inland a few miles from the beach and has a much larger population. The music style was mainly blues and early rock. The blues bands would occasionally draw some unattached solo musicians, who, if they were good enough, would sit in and join the scheduled band for a set or two.

"Who's playing this weekend, Tommy?" I asked.

"If my memory serves me correctly, I believe it is Attitude Blue." replied Tom. "Maybe someone will join them and help to uplift the quality of the musical entertainment just a touch."

Tom was a real character. He came from a very refined family in Charleston, South Carolina. He had gone to college at Clemson where he earned a Bachelor's degree in English Literature and had gotten about halfway through the Master's program in the same field before he lost interest and became a bartender. Tom's accent was a blend of old Southern gentry with a British twist. Not your typical guy drawing drafts back there. When it came to academic knowledge, he was deep. As a rule, Tom took an intellectual slant on things, which made for some interesting contrasts with the regular clientele at the Blue Moon. He was single and usually worked long hours, six days a week, with only Mondays off. The Blue Moon was pretty much Tom's life.

The bar mostly drew a local crowd with a bit of a harder edge to them. Tourists would occasionally patronize the place, but they usually didn't appear comfortable. There were many other establishments on the island more attractive to the vacationers' dollar. The Blue Moon was a drinking bar.

"Well, I'll be in on Friday night and take in a set or two," I said. "Let me have one more, Tommy, and then I will chauffeur Mr. Forte home."

"Coming up," said Tom, pulling the tall

wooden tap that was shaped and painted in the form of a palm tree.

Roger Carson called from across the bar, "Are you boys still on for the fishing trip on Monday?"

"Yessiree," I said.

"I shall be in attendance," Tom answered.

"I guess I'll just have to show you guys a thing or two about how to catch fish," added Harry.

"Oh," replied Roger, "aren't we so lucky to have an expert coming along to teach all of us the finer points of fishing."

"I'll give Wayne a call," I said, "to see if he can make it. But I'll be surprised if he takes a day off from earning his latest fortune to grace us with his company."

Wayne McMillan was a realtor for Forte Real Estate, one of the largest operations in Southwest Florida. Interestingly, Harry Forte's father was the founder and president of the firm. Harry had never gotten involved with the company, saying he just didn't like the idea of selling anything, especially real estate. Harry and Wayne McMillan had been friends since they were kids. They also had been classmates in high school up in the City of St. George. Wayne had worked in some capacity for the elder Forte since graduation. In the beginning, he had done maintenance work on some of the commercial properties, but it was quickly apparent he had the gift of gab and the motivation to do the salesman thing. Both Wayne and Harry were twenty-eight, but their lives had taken two distinctly different paths over the previous ten years. Wayne was driven.

Money was a huge motivator for him and he'd put in countless hours to obtain it. He worked in the commercial end of the business during the week and then showed residential real estate on weekends. Obtaining wealth was what life was all about for Wayne McMillan.

Harry, on the other hand, had rejected that type of lifestyle. He worked for a nursery that supplied palm trees and shrubbery. He drove a tractor with a flatbed trailer and also operated a forklift for unloading and placing the trees. He was a bull of a man and loved the physical part of the work. It was no surprise to anyone that a white-collar job was not for him.

"It doesn't make any difference, either way," said Roger Carson. "It'll be four of us without him, or five with."

I finished my beer, paid the tab, and said, "Let's go, Harry. I'm giving you a ride home."

"Now wait just a minute, El," started Harry.

"Aw, go on, Harry," a voice called from the front of the bar. I swung around and in the doorway stood Wayne McMillan. "You better let the nice man drive you home," said Wayne.

"Speak of the devil, Wayne," I said. "We were just wondering if you were going to join us on Monday to go fishing on Roger's boat."

"Wouldn't miss it," said Wayne as he took a stool at the bar. He was impeccably dressed, as usual. Tan linen suit with Gucci loafers and not a hair out of place. It looked like he had just stepped out of a GQ magazine ad. When he had business on the island, he would often stop by the Blue Moon late in the afternoon for his own personal happy hour.

"Alright, Roger," I called, "the total is five for Monday."

"Gotcha," said Roger.

"Okay, Harry," I said, standing, "the taxi's leaving. Let's go." Then to the rest, "See you guys later."

"Adieu, gentlemen," called Tom the bartender.

"See you two later," said Wayne. "And, Ellis, be real careful with that precious cargo you've got there."

Harry and I walked across the parking lot of the Blue Moon, which consisted of crushed seashells. Next to Harry's pickup was Wayne McMillan's white BMW sedan. It must have been the biggest model they made. The car was enormous. It had every option know to man. Everything but running water, Wayne liked to say. I unlocked my bike from the rack and put it in the bed of Harry's pickup. The truck was a compact style that didn't seem suited for Harry's size. You had to wonder how he even fit in it. Just as I was getting in the driver's side, I saw Harry take a couple of quick steps toward the passenger door calling, "Check this out, I'm a NASCAR driver." He flung his huge body toward the truck, and with his feet leading the way, tried to slide through the open window. Somewhere between his waist and chest, the attempt came to an abrupt halt. He was stuck. I had twisted my shoulders and head just in time to miss getting a size thirteen boot to the jaw. His other foot caught the rearview mirror and snapped it like a twig off of the windshield. I got out of the pickup, walked around to the other side, and broke into hysterical laughter. The sight of Harry Forte stuck halfway in and halfway out of the window was almost more than a body could bear.

"Oh boy, you went and done it now, Harry," I barely got out in between laughs. "What the hell were you doing anyway? You almost took my head off."

"Get me out of here, Ellis," pleaded Harry. "I'm stuck, man."

"Sure thing, Harry. Let me go get some help." I walked around to the doorway of the Blue Moon and announced to all assembled, "If you folks would like to have your day made, please accompany me to the parking lot. You're not going to believe it."

Wayne, Roger and a couple of other guys leaped up from their stools and piled down the front steps behind me. On the way, I heard Tom announce in a loud voice to the patrons that remained, "This bar is temporarily on hold," as he hustled out after us.

A roar of hooting and hollering erupted in the parking lot. I would imagine the scene of the six or seven of us doubled over was as funny and silly as what we were laughing at. Harry was a round peg stuck in a square hole. After an appropriate amount of hilarity, a couple of the guys grabbed him under his arms, and with me pushing his legs from inside the pickup, Harry finally popped out.

Barely getting the words out from laughing, Wayne said, "Harry, next time you're going to try a stunt like that, let me know so I can round up every-body I have ever known."

"I'm all right, man," said Harry, checking himself for injuries.

"Yeah, you're sure all right, big guy," said Wayne, in clear amusement.

Order was finally restored and the others, still laughing, returned to the bar. Harry and I got back into his truck the conventional way. I started it up, pulled out of the lot, and headed south on Calusa Boulevard. It's the main drag of St. George Beach, running the entire length. The island is a relatively thin strip of land about seven miles long with many side streets. Calusa Bay separates the island from the mainland. Both the Boulevard and the Bay were named after the Calusa Indian tribe, which had in-habited the island centuries earlier. Behind a number of the residential properties are canals that afford ac-cess to the back bay.

Harry lived with his wife, Brenda, in a small ranch house near the middle of the island. They didn't have children. Brenda worked at an upscale clothing store in the City of St. George. Her job re-quired working many hours in the evening and on weekends. With Harry working during the daytime on weekdays, there wasn't a lot of time they spent together, at least awake. I had heard it said by oth-ers that their conflicting work schedule was the main reason they got along.

I pulled the pickup into Harry's driveway,

parked it, and dropped the keys into the palm of his open hand. After we got out, Harry pulled his tee shirt up to examine his torso.

"You've got some pretty nice scrapes and scratches there, my boy," I said. "Next time I think you ought to use the door."

"Yeah, good idea, Ellis," said Harry. "You're always thinking. Thanks for the ride. Even though I know I could have done it." He then turned and shuffled toward his front door.

I took my bike out of Harry's pickup and we waved goodbye as I rode off. As I pedaled down the Boulevard, I was still laughing to myself about his ridiculous bid to leap through the truck window. If there was ever an opportunity to show off, Harry would always jump at the chance. In this case, literally. Regardless of the outcome, he never failed to make an impression.

I live about a mile south on the island from Harry's place. When I got home, I unlocked the garage and put my bike inside. Over the years, I had acquired a total of six refrigerators that I had hooked up in the garage. They served as cold storage for my inventory of supplies for the vendor cart. I had run extra electric lines to the garage and had spaced outlets around the perimeter. I even had a commercial icemaker. The place looked like the appliance department at Sears. I always watched the classified ads for used refrigerators. When you're in my business, you can never have enough of them.

I went in the house, took a shower, and put on a tan sport shirt and a clean pair of jean shorts. At seven o'clock I was meeting my friend, Marie, for our standard Wednesday night get-together. Now don't get the wrong idea. Our relationship was not your typical dating, leading to commitment, kind of thing. I had known Marie for about two and a half years. I met her when she was a waitress at the Beer Garden restaurant on Calusa Boulevard. She had come to Florida from Brazil with her mother when she was a young child. Her real name was Maria but she had changed it to "Americanize" herself. She was twenty-six and the single mother of five-year-old Sandra who was a carbon copy of Marie. They both had dark hair, dark eyes, a pretty face, and the most beautiful skin you could ever imagine. They lived in a small apartment only a few blocks from my house.

Although Marie and I were attracted to each other, we did not share the same goals for a happy existence. Marie yearned for the good life and she was smart enough to have a plan to obtain it. She intended to marry either a man on the way up, or one who had already gained financial security. She had changed waitress jobs many times, with each succeeding restaurant being nicer than the one before. She was now working at the Fountainhead, which was a new hotel and convention center on St. George Beach. It was, and always had been, Marie's ambition to meet a man with money and let nature take it course. She figured working at a place the wealthy patronized was her ticket to meeting Mr. Right. It was obvious to both of us, I was not that guy. I had happily operated my vendor cart for the previous sixteen years and I had no intention of making a career change. Even considering the differing views, our relationship was one of friendship and convenience. As an added benefit for both of us, the needs of the flesh were fulfilled, if only on a weekly basis. We both knew, realistically, our arrangement was temporary. Neither of us had a big problem with that.

Each Wednesday we walked to dinner at the Beer Garden. Marie had an elderly woman for a neighbor who kept Sandra overnight when we went out. For Sandra, the matronly babysitter served as a surrogate grandmother. Everyone was happy with the arrangement. A little before seven, I walked to Marie's apartment. As I ascended the outside wooden steps to her second floor door, a light breeze made the fronds of the surrounding palm trees chatter. I knocked lightly and in a moment Marie came to the door. She was wearing a bright colored blouse that had a flowery print, and khaki shorts. She looked very nice. Heck, she could have been wearing dirty old clothes and she would still look nice as far as I was concerned. She rarely wore makeup and I liked that. There was a natural beauty about her that really didn't need any artificial improvement.

"Good evening, pretty Miss," I said.

She smiled and said, "Good evening, yourself."

"All set?" I said.

"Yeah, let's go."

The traffic on Calusa Boulevard was light as we crossed. Not the parking lot it became during the season. We cut between two high-rise condominiums to get out on the beach. There was only a little over an hour before sunset and the low angle of the sun cast long shadows of us on one of the walls as we passed between the buildings. As we walked north, close to the Gulf, small shells crunched beneath our sandals. The air was lighter at this boundary between land and water. A sort of cleansing for the mind and body at the edge of the map. The serenity was momentarily interrupted as a flock of screeching seagulls flew past us and headed down the beach.

When we got to the Beer Garden, we went around to the front and up several steps to the deck. The owner, Luis Perez, greeted us saying, "Ah, it's easy now, my friends." He hugged each of us and then led us to a table on the deck with a close-up view of the beach and Gulf. Luis had a natural talent for making customers feel welcome. He tailored his style depending on their age and demeanor, as well as his familiarity with the diners. He seemed to know how to press all the right buttons to get a positive response. It was very easy for anyone to feel comfortable and appreciated at his restaurant.

"It's so good to see you both, as usual," he said seating us. "Now Marie, can't I get you to come back and work here again? The customers are asking for you all the time. Oh, I know you've made it up to the big time at the Fountainhead, but I'll keep trying to convince you anyway. We miss you here."

This was a plea that Luis made almost every time we were at the Beer Garden. He was persistent in that regard. I don't think that he really expected Marie to actually come back, but it was his way to make her feel wanted and valued.

"That's very nice for you to say, Luis," said Marie. "I miss the people here, too. But it's onward and upward, you know."

"Okay, for now," said Luis, "but I won't stop trying. Now you two lovely people enjoy your meal."

A steel drum band returned to the deck from their break and began playing music of the islands. Listening to the tropical sounds and looking out over the Gulf was very relaxing. We enjoyed a dinner of grilled chicken strips over black beans and yellow rice. We also shared a carafe of white wine with the dinner. Our waitress delivered two glasses of water with the wine. Luis instructed his wait staff to always serve water with wine. He was a real stickler for detail and felt that water was an essential partner to wine.

"How did the luncheon at the hotel go today?" I asked.

"Oh, it was just the Chamber of Commerce meeting," said Marie. "You know, all of the old blowhards trying to outdo each other. Most of them just like to hear themselves talk."

"So I guess there wasn't any potential man of your dreams in that group, huh."

"Why do you always bug me about that?" she said. "I'll land what I'm looking for one of these days. I think about my future and about Sandra. What's wrong with that?"

"There's nothing wrong with that. I'm sorry. I was just kidding you."

"I mean, look at you. You had a chance to make it. You could have been some hotshot pharmacist up north making lots of dough. Just because you want to spend the rest of your life peddling hot dogs and sodas doesn't mean you're right or I'm wrong."

"Okay, Marie, easy, easy," I said. "I'm doing what I want to do, and I'm happy with it. Money's not that big a deal with me. I know you've got Sandra and I don't blame you for trying for a better life. That's no crime. I know you'll meet somebody. I hope it works out for you. I really do." I held out my wine glass, and with a small smile she toasted me.

"Thanks," she said, "I'm only trying to do what I think is right."

We finished our meal, paid the bill, and said our goodbyes to Luis. As usual, he was the gracious host and said he couldn't wait for us to come back. As we walked down the beach, the sun was setting. Rays of light glistened across the small ripples on the Gulf. And colorful hues of orange and pink were developing on puffy clouds above. We stopped and took in the whole scene. It was beautiful. An older couple wearing bathing suits was frolicking in the Gulf water up to their waists. Everyone had his or her own way of enjoying the daily sunset ritual. I turned to Marie and said, "I meant what I said at dinner. I really do want—"

"Ellis, Ellis," she said in earnest. Marie's face had a frightened, panicked look to it. "Something's not right out there."

I turned and saw the woman of the older pair struggling to lift the man by his armpits. He had collapsed in several feet of water. The woman began urgently calling for help. I took off toward them, kicking off my sandals before I reached the water. Another guy, who had been photographing the sunset, put down his camera and joined me. When the two of us got to the man in trouble and tried to pull him up it was like lifting a dead weight. It took a tenacious effort by both of us to get him onto the beach. All the time, the woman kept crying, "Eddie, oh, Eddie."

Eddie was unconscious when we got him out of the water but his eyes had not rolled back. A woman, who was walking on the beach, ran over and started to perform CPR. In between breaths, water flowed out of the man's mouth. In the meantime, Marie ran back across the wide beach toward the condominiums. On a number of the balconies were people watching the sunset. Marie frantically yelled for someone to call 911. Meanwhile, the woman who was giving the CPR was relieved by a younger fellow, and after what seemed like an eternity, I heard sirens in the distance.

Moments later, I saw the circular flashing of red lights between the condo buildings. With the close spacing of the high-rises, plus the surrounding landscaping, there wasn't enough room to drive the ambulance out onto the beach. Finally, two paramedics appeared on foot, but they didn't run or seem hurried. With a lot of equipment in hand, they walked to the scene purposefully and methodically. I guess they wanted to have their wits about them when they got to the spot of the emergency. Marie encouraged them along and even asked if she could carry anything for them, but they declined. When the EMTs arrived, they set up their various medical devices and proceeded to attend to the man. It seemed likely he had sustained a heart attack. Ironically, he would have died of drowning had we not yanked him out of the water. Based on the effort it took the two of us guys, there was no way the woman could have gotten Eddie up on the beach by herself.

After a short time, I realized the situation was in better hands and suggested to Marie that we leave. As I looked back at the activity one last time I noticed, by mere coincidence, my sandals were lying just in front of the victim's feet. I made my way through the circle of onlookers that had gathered and, almost with embarrassment, picked them up. I didn't want people to think I was taking the poor guy's sandals.

As Marie and I walked back off the beach we were speechless. We just glanced at each other in stunned silence. After we crossed the Boulevard, we walked down to a nearby liquor store. I bought a small bottle of Kahlua and one of vodka. When we got back to Marie's apartment, I mixed up a couple of White Russians. We sipped on them and they helped us to unwind a little from the stressful episode we had just gone through. After an event like that, we both agreed that you just never know about things that can happen in life. As was our custom, I stayed the night and left early in the morning.

When I got back to my house, I called the Rescue Patrol station and inquired about the condition of the man from the night before. I was told that when he was delivered to the hospital, he was alive. They didn't have any other information on him. I had a feeling of relief that at least he didn't die right there on the beach. He must have had a guardian angel looking after him, because another minute or two in the water and he would have been gone. It was an odd set of circumstances that on a fairly deserted beach, several unrelated parties combined their efforts to help save him.

I put on my bathing suit and went over to the beach for my morning swim. It felt a little eerie getting in the water considering what had happened the previous evening, but after a few minutes I was back in the swing of things. I swam north, parallel to the beach, for fifteen minutes and then turned around and retraced my path. On the return trip, several dolphins, with their backs repetitively breaking the surface of the water, passed me just a few yards away. If we were in a race, I wouldn't stand a chance against those guys. It gave me a good feeling that man and nature could coexist so closely. In this case, however, I was on *their* turf, so to speak.

Then it was back to the house and a quick rinse-off in my outdoor shower before I loaded up the vendor cart for the day. A few years back, the old Opel finally died on me and I bought a used white '83 Chevy Van to haul the cart. It wasn't much to look at, but it did the job. It also served as a sort of mobile warehouse to haul extra supplies. I made my way on up to my beach access spot. I had a deal with the attendant at the parking lot directly across the Boulevard. He'd let me park my van in his lot every day at no charge, in exchange for a couple of hot dogs and a soda for lunch. It wasn't really fair. I mean, I was getting free parking and he was destroying his body with the toxic junk I gave him to eat. But he always seemed very happy about the arrangement. He made it clear he thought it was great. As the saying goes, "give 'em what they want."

As I was getting set up for business, Frank Olivetti came by with his push-along vendor cart. He was the guy I had worked for on the beach the one summer during high school, and again for a time when I first came to live with my grandmother. Frank was in his fifties but you would never know it by his build. He had always been a weight-lifting fanatic. I'm telling you, the guy's piped. Frank belonged to the gym on Calusa Boulevard and every morning he'd lift weights for a couple of hours. He was the perennial champ in his weight class at all of the local lifting competitions. On the beach, he really stood out. Frank was recognizable not only by his physique, but by the way he had his cart decorated. He had a pole, fashioned into a palm tree, which extended up from his cart about six or seven feet. From the top of the tree was a stuffed monkey hanging on by one hand. The monkey would sway back and forth as the cart went along. At the midpoint of the pole, a wooden dowel stuck out. It served as a perch for Frank's pet parrot. Not a stuffed one, mind you, a real live parrot. It had the brightest and most varied colors I had ever seen.

Frank was the hit of the beach, especially with kids. He'd go along ringing a string of bells similar to the old-time ice cream vendors. Kids would run up to him to get a closer look at the parrot. Frank would take the bird down and show everyone by using his finger as a perch. He really liked to pose for pictures with that parrot. Frank was proud of both the parrot and of the muscular body he had carved at the gym for the world to see. He was also very popular with the pretty young girls, and that suited Frank just fine. With all of his various enticements, he was a magnet for business. He did have several young guys working for him with other carts on the beach, but he consistently outsold them. Even though Frank and I were in the same business, we never thought of each other as being in competition for customers. I got 'em going to and from the beach, and they were his while they were there.

"Yo, what's up today, Ellis?" called Frank.

"Oh, not much, yet," I said, "but we did have a little excitement last night on the beach just below the Beer Garden." As I proceeded to give Frank a brief description of what had transpired, he stood there shaking his head.

"Man, oh, man," he said, "never a dull moment around here, huh?"

"No sir. Just a real quiet little paradise," I replied. "Every day is like Sunday on the farm."

"Well, off I go a' vending," Frank said. "I've got to get out there and slave-drive those boys pushing my other carts. You know, give them a little pep talk. I've got to watch them like a hawk with the inventory, too, or they'll rob me blind."

"See, that's what you get for being such a

big time entrepreneur. I only have little ol' me to worry about."

"See you, Ellis. Have fun."

"Take care, big guy."

A little past noon, I looked up from the sports page when I heard the toot of a car horn. Waving from her cream-colored Jaguar convertible was Lisa McMillan, Wayne's wife. She was pulling into the parking lot across the street. After getting a beach bag and sand chair out of the trunk, she walked on the opposite sidewalk toward the crosswalk. Lisa was not what you would describe as beautiful, but she was certainly attractive. She was blonde and slender with a sculpted figure. Lisa had on a skimpy white bikini, a floral sarong wraparound, and white high-heeled sandals. You couldn't miss her.

One of the traffic laws on the island is that cars have to yield to pedestrians at various intervals along Calusa Boulevard. The crosswalks are marked with signs and flashing lights. Still, the wise thing to do is at least make some kind of eye contact with oncoming drivers before you step into the street. Not Lisa. She boldly started across without looking either way. Sure enough, a car, with a driver not paying attention, squealed to a stop within a couple of feet of her. After cursing and making a gesture to the guy behind the wheel, Lisa continued across the Boulevard. She was shaking her head as she approached my cart.

"Do you believe that jerk?" said Lisa, clearly irritated. "He almost ran me over."

"Yeah, I saw the whole thing," I said. "He must have had his eyes closed. People don't pay attention to those signs. You really have to be careful and make sure they're going to stop."

"Man, I don't believe it," she said. Then her upset demeanor completely vanished. With a broad smile, she said, "So how are you today, Ellis?" The way Lisa could switch on the charm made you question her sincerity when she spoke to you.

"Oh, fine," I replied, "another day another dollar, you know."

"Just selling up a storm of the old hot dogs and sausages, eh?" Lisa was still smiling but I got the distinct impression she was being critical of my chosen profession.

"Everything's going fine. Not a care in the world."

Lisa looked toward the beach and said, "It's pretty breezy down here today. I may rent one of those chaises with the wind blockers."

"Yeah, you don't want to have any sand blowing on you while you're getting your tan, now do you?" I said, smiling. "By the way, Wayne says he's going out with us for a little fishing venture on Monday." The expression on her face went blank and immediately I knew I had said the wrong thing. I could tell she didn't know anything about the fishing trip.

"Oh, is that right?" she said. "He's really close to closing a deal on the new professional building up in town. It's going to mean a big fat commission. I wouldn't think he'd want to take time away from that project."

"Oh, I bet one day wouldn't hurt. And, anyway, you guys aren't hurting for grocery money," I said with a laugh.

"Now, Ellis, you can't have too much of the green. Besides, I've got my eye on a new houseboat down at Gateway Marina. It has this big canopy over the back half. It'd be great to have parties on. It's the best."

"I bet it is."

"Look, I've got to get going," she said. "See you."

"Take it easy, Lisa," I said as she strutted off.

It was tough getting Lisa off of my mind for a while. For one thing, dealing with her materialism was like drinking vinegar. Plus, she was so judgmental about both people and things. Everything had to be "the best." The best, the best, the best. That expression kills me. To me, it's saying something is without peer. It's saying there's no competitive product that comes close. I don't buy that. Isn't it really just an opinion most of the time? To say something's the best makes you sound like you're a stinking authority. Like nobody can question your judgment unless they're ready for an argument. Lisa could really get under your skin. Man, she was materialistic. I imagine it could be said, if it bothered me so much, I was probably just being jealous. I don't know. I guess it has to do with your point of view. I think it's more of what you value. I'm happy living here in paradise. Freedom and friendships are the things that are important to me. You can't put a price tag on watching a stunning sunset. You can't buy a beautiful day. To Lisa, the more something cost, the better it was. The better it was, the more she wanted it. That way of thinking seemed shallow to me.

I think the thing that bothered me most was her influence on Wayne. I'd known Wayne through Harry Forte for four or five years, and we had become good friends. Wayne had a contagious smile and was fun to be around. Now don't get me wrong. Wayne liked having the nicer things, for sure. He had been raised in an average middle-class environment, but he had always strived to do better. His objective was to move up. To gain wealth and status. He was ambitious and he had the work ethic to go with it. He had never minded putting in long hours to earn money he could throw around. It wasn't that Wayne was a showoff. He just wanted to do the things rich people did and have the things rich people had, and he was willing to work hard for it. The problem was, as I saw it, being married to Lisa was like pouring gasoline on the fire. She bled every ounce of effort from him. Work more. Earn more. Wayne said she would start every sentence with, "I need." I bet the whole deal wouldn't have bugged me quite as much if she worked, too. When it came to making money, Wayne was the one who carried the ball.

Wayne and Lisa had been married for a little over three years. They had not yet had any children. Oh, Lisa talked a good game about wanting to have a baby. I think she looked at it as having yet another possession. Deep down, however, I didn't think she wanted one at all. My take on the subject was, (a) she didn't want to commit to the responsibility, (b) she didn't want to lose her self-centered independence, and (c) she didn't want to mess up her shapely figure. Appearances were a big item with Lisa. Her image in other people's eyes was something I believed she thought about constantly. It is said that politicians are very concerned with posturing. Man, when it came to posturing, Lisa wrote the book.

It had been a pretty slow day, so I closed up a little early and hauled the cart back to my house. I grabbed a couple of granola bars and a bottle of water and put them in one of the baskets on my bike. I had attached three baskets of various sizes to the good old beach cruiser. I could carry a ton of cargo on her. When I had her really filled, I kind of looked like one of those mobile vagabonds. I got my fishing gear together, loaded up, and headed south down Calusa Boulevard. I pulled into Gateway Marina and picked up some live shrimp for bait. I asked the guy in the tackle shop about the houseboat Lisa had described to me. He pointed it out and, as I was leaving the lot, I rode by where it was on display. The thing was really swanked out. Although I hadn't asked, I figured it probably cost as much or more than what my house was worth. Oh well, to each his own.

Off I went down to the bridge over Gateway Pass. The late afternoon sun was beaming and the earlier breeze had calmed. I locked my bike to a light pole at the bottom of the bridge and, with quite an effort, carried everything up to the top. There's a fairly wide paved walkway on both sides and fishing from the bridge is very popular. The speed limit for crossing vehicles is reduced to twenty-five miles an hour. The apparent rationale is to help protect the fishermen from getting clipped by speeding drivers. The apex of the bridge is about thirty feet above the water. It's high enough for some pretty-good-sized boats to go underneath. As I mentioned earlier, the view from atop the bridge is awesome. I mean, I've never been to the Grand Canyon, but the sight of Gateway Pass opening up into the Gulf of Mexico is a vista that's good enough for me.

I set up shop at an open spot on the Gulf side of the bridge and baited my hook with a live shrimp. I lowered the line down into the water and then just gazed around and took in the scenery. To the south of Gateway Pass is a large undeveloped park area. From the base of the bridge to the park entrance there was road construction in progress. A number of temporary concrete barriers were set up to channel traffic as the road curved southward. The park itself consists of a series of mangrove islands that are separated by small tributaries leading either to the Gulf of Mexico or to Calusa Bay. Very primitive. It is probably just about the same as it had been hundreds of years ago. Maybe now the islands are a little bigger.

The mangroves are really interesting. They

have this extensive root system that particles of dirt, leaves, pollen, or whatever attach themselves to. Over time, the whole thing slowly grows bigger, creating land. To make a long story short, if you stuck the roots of a mangrove into some shallow water and came back in a few thousand years, you'd have a big ol' island.

By fishing off of the bridge once or twice a week, I tended to see a lot of the same faces. But no one got too chummy, though, and I didn't ever learn people's names. There was, however, a kind of camaraderie amongst the regulars. Folks were polite and said hello to each other, but nobody wanted to know your business. I like that. If you want to talk, go to a bar. Fishing is more of a quiet, personal deal. At least, that's the way I look at it.

After about ten minutes, I got a tug on my line, set the hook, and started to reel in. As I pulled

the line up out of the water, I saw that I had hooked a sheepshead. It's one of the more common fish you could expect to catch off the bridge. Just before I got it up to the railing, it flipped off of the hook and dropped back down into the Pass.

"Come back, little Sheba," I yelled.

"Looks like that one got away from you," called the angler who was ten or fifteen yards down on my left.

"Oh, well," I said, "there's more where that came from."

Besides sheepshead, you could anticipate catching Spanish mackerel, trout or redfish off the bridge. If you had a boat and ventured out into the Gulf, other larger varieties of fish are waiting. The whole area of Southwest Florida is truly a world-class fisherman's haven. Looking for an impressive natural fisherman? It has to be the osprey. That bird is similar in appearance to an eagle, but maybe a little less majestic. They nest on the tops of trees and also on manmade platforms and light standards. The osprey can fly along, then swoop down and, with their talons, grab a fish right out of the water. It's something to see. As a kid, I had never done much fishing, but while living on St. George Beach I had gotten the bug. I wasn't totally devoted to it and all that, but for me, fishing is relaxing recreation. The added benefit is catching food I enjoy eating.

I stayed on the bridge for a couple of hours. After I caught two keeper redfish, I packed up. The main course for dinner was in my cooler and I was satisfied. I liked being on that bridge so much that

I would have been just about as happy if I hadn't caught anything.

I rode back up the Boulevard, and after picking up some fresh vegetables at the local market, I went home. I put everything away and then went into the garage to do my inventory count. Every Thursday, in the early evening, I would always check all of my supplies for the cart. I'd count up the hot dogs, sausages, sodas, bagels, fruit, you name it. I would make up an order and then call this guy who is my supplier. Each Friday morning, he drives his truck down to my house and makes a delivery. Doing the inventory thing on Thursday has always been standard procedure for me. It's like clockwork.

When I was done, I went into the kitchen and turned on the radio to the jazz station from up in St. George. I opened a bottle of beer and cleaned the two fish I'd caught. My plan was to make dinner and go to bed early because I was probably going to go out Friday night to hear some music at the Blue Moon.

# 6

After work on Friday I came straight home. Since the bands usually didn't start playing until around eight o'clock, I thought I'd relax for a couple of hours. I got something to eat, showered, and put on a clean tee shirt and jean shorts. Except for the nights I went out with Marie, my attire remained extremely casual. Shoot, I didn't want to be mistaken for a tourist by wearing some fancy-ass duds. That's a dead giveaway. Especially at the Blue Moon. No doubt, I'd be razzed by the regulars if I pulled a stunt like that.

I stepped out the back door and sat on a recliner on the small patio. I always felt very at ease there. I could check out the canal that ran behind my house. There were a few neighbors who had sizeable boats behind their properties. A couple of them even had an elaborate pulley system to raise their boats completely out of the water. I only had a little twelve-foot runabout. Sometimes I'd take the Minnow, as I called her, through the canal and out into Calusa Bay to go fishing. Other times I'd fish right off of my patio. Believe it or not, what I thought was the most fun was to just sit back there and watch the water in the canal for leaping mullet. Fairly often, one would break the surface and fly airborne a foot or two out of the water. Sometimes even higher. The fish would then splash irreverently back into the canal. It might sound like a simple pleasure, but I never got tired of it. I looked at it as a display of aquatic acrobatics.

At about seven-thirty, I drove my van up to the Blue Moon. If I were going to be out well after dark, I'd usually drive rather than ride my bike. That is, except during January, February, and March. The traffic, as previously noted, is horrendous during the season. It seems like a game has just let out, constantly. The streams of traffic are relentless. Good for business, lousy for getting around. If you wanted to drive anywhere on the island during those months you had to do it early in the morning. I would always allow plenty of extra minutes for possible and probable delays on my commute to the beach access in the wintertime. Wintertime. That's a good one. Not the standard scraping of the windshield and shoveling of snow here in paradise. In the winter, however, my extensive and extravagant wardrobe would usually switch to regular jeans and long sleeve tee shirts. I will even don a sweatshirt, or sometimes two. After a while, you become so acclimated to the warmth that a sixty-five degree day in January can seem chilly. But it still beats the heck out of the winters up in Pennsylvania by a mile.

I walked into the Blue Moon and took a stool where I could get a good look at the stage. If I was going to listen to live music, I wanted to be able to see the band. The place was about half full. Since it was Friday, more of a crowd was bound to roll in as the night wore on. Tom Grissom was behind the bar.

"What's going on, Tommy?" I said.

"Same old itinerary, Ellis," said Tom. "You make a request, and I get it for you."

"In that case, I'll have a draft."

"At your service."

I saw Roger Carson sitting across the bar and we exchanged waves. Roger was kind of a loner. He was a friendly enough guy, but he generally sat by himself and observed the bar scene. Maybe all those

41

years as a charter boat captain had worn out some of his social skills. I would imagine that putting up with tremendous numbers of drunken fishermen, and remaining tactful and diplomatic, could be trying. Having been out on his boat for so long, his face had tons of lines and creases from the sun and wind. It looked like a nautical map. You know, I'd never seen him drunk. He always paced himself and the beer level in his glass never seemed to change. I decided that one night I was going to do a study on him and keep track of how many beers he actually did drink. This was not the night.

A few members of the band had arrived and they were setting up their equipment. I'd seen Attitude Blue a couple of times before and their music was a little above the modest average of what the Blue Moon usually booked. I noticed the band's leader back in the corner of the bar sitting at a table with a young black musician who was wearing a suit and tie. I'd never seen the younger guy before. He was playing his unplugged electric guitar for the guy from the band. I couldn't hear what he was playing due to the music blaring from the jukebox, but I could see the quickness of his hand speed.

"Looks like somebody's getting an audition back there, Tommy."

"Indeed," said Tom. "I don't believe I've seen that young gentleman before."

"Well, I don't know if he sounds any good," I said, "but his hands move like lightning."

"It looks like we're going to get a chance to find out," said Tom, nodding toward the corner.

The head guy of Attitude Blue and the young fellow were standing and shaking hands. The black guitarist was slightly built and couldn't have been more than five-foot-three or four. As he moved over toward the stage I got a better look at him. He appeared even younger than I had first thought, possibly still in his teens. He had delicate facial features and, with the way he was sharply dressed, he carried with him a certain refinement. My analysis of the guy was suddenly and boldly interrupted by a monstrous slap on my back. It was Harry Forte. If I had been taking a drink at the time, I would have been wearing my beer.

"What's happening?" yelled Harry over the music from the jukebox, as he sat down on the stool next to me.

"Let me get the air you just knocked out of me back in my lungs and I'll let you know," I barked.

"Yeah, man," said Harry. "Hey, Tommy, how about a draft over here."

"One moment, your highness," called Tom with a sarcastic tone as he bowed in Harry's direction.

"Did you recover from Wednesday?" I asked Harry. "You had a real rum-dumb thing going."

"Yeah, I was a little smashed, but no big deal," said Harry. "I got a couple of nice bruises on my back, though, from the door lock."

I gestured toward the stage and said, "Hey, check out this little guy that's setting up with the band. He just got hired a few minutes ago. I'm not sure, but I think he might be pretty good."

Harry looked over toward the stage and then turned back saying, "I think I saw that guy at Cleo's up in St. George last weekend and he wasn't too good."

"Really?"

"Yeah, man, he couldn't keep up with the rest of the band he was playing with."

"Huh," I said.

A little after eight, the jukebox was turned off and the soft lights over the stage came on. The bandleader, who also played guitar, stepped up to the microphone.

"Good evening, everybody, we are Attitude Blue. Tonight, as an extra treat, we have added a new guitar player. His name is Luther Haynes, but he likes to be called Lil' Luther. Let's everybody give him a warm welcome."

There was light applause. The Blue Moon clientele was not normally the most enthusiastic audience. They kind of had a "show me what you got" attitude. The group started out the first set with a Freddie King instrumental "Hideaway." Lil' Luther hit the ground running. He could play. As I had suspected, he had quick hands, but he also had an impressive command of the notes. It seemed like the rest of the band were the ones having a little trouble keeping up with him. Just the opposite of what Harry had said a few minutes earlier.

When the song finished, Harry turned to me and said, "Different guy than I saw last weekend." When it became apparent that Harry was wrong about something after having made a bold statement, he'd drop the subject quickly and cleanly.

The band followed up with a song written by Sonny Thompson, "I'm Tore Down," which had also been recorded by the legendary Freddie King. Lil' Luther proved he could sing, too. He ripped though it with ease. In the Freddie King distinctive manner, Luther played with authority and confidence. It gave the impression that he'd sat down and figured out every note ahead of time, but he seemed so relaxed, the whole presentation just flowed along. The words of the song expressed unbounded devotion to the singer's woman. But when Luther pined away with the repeated lines, "Well I'm tore down; I'm almost level with the ground/Well I feel like this when my baby can't be found," he brought a believable, yet sorrowful, meaning to it.

Boy, the band got a warm reception after that number. Loud applause. I think everyone quickly realized they were in for some powerful entertainment. It was amazing that a young guy like Lil' Luther possessed such skill and style. He was smooth as silk. From a visual standpoint, Luther certainly stood out. He, of course, was small, black, and dressed in a tailored suit. The rest of the band consisted of big white guys in jeans and tee shirts. It made for an odd look, but in blues bands, race and style of clothes really doesn't mean much. How well you can play, does. There was no doubt Attitude Blue had moved up the musical ladder more than a few rungs with the addition of Lil' Luther. Breezing through the first set, Luther showed song after song he could both play guitar and sing. In addition, it became apparent he was well versed on the harmonica, also known as the blues harp. The guy had talent.

# 7

When the band took a break, I waved Tom over. As he was drawing Harry and me another beer, I said, "Well, I'd have to say Lil' Luther can flat-out play, Tommy."

"Indeed he can." said Tom. "More musical ability than I believe I've ever seen in this establishment."

"Man," said Harry, "the little guy can cook."

"Those two beers are on me, Tommy," called a voice from over my shoulder. It was Wayne McMillan sitting down on the barstool to my right. He was dressed in a stylish Italian suit that he'd probably had on all day, but you would never have known it. Like always, he looked fresh as a daisy. "And I'll have Absolut on the rocks with olives," said Wayne.

"Thank you, sir," I said.

"Yeah, thanks, Wayne," said Harry.

"So, Wayne," I said, "what brings you out to this old watering hole at nine o'clock on a Friday night?"

"I just had dinner with this guy who's a developer. I'm trying to swing a deal with him on some real estate down at the south end of the island. He wants to build some condos," said Wayne, rubbing his thumb and forefinger together. "He's got big bucks. Could be a tidy commission in store if I can work the thing out."

"Ah, you're never one to miss out on an opportunity now are you?" I said.

"There you go, my good man," said Tom as he set the cocktail down in front of Wayne.

"Thanks, Tommy, take their beers and my drink out of this," said Wayne as he handed Tom a fifty-dollar bill.

Harry leaned backward and, speaking over my shoulder, said to Wayne, "How's my old man doing? I haven't talked to him in a couple of weeks."

"Doing fine," said Wayne, "he's been real busy, you know, like always."

"Wayne," I said, "you've gotta hear this guy playing tonight. He's tearing it up."

"When I was getting out of the car," said Wayne, "I heard the tail end of the last song. It sounded pretty good."

"He's real good," said Harry.

"So you're out working on Friday night," I said. "Don't you ever give it a break?"

"Hey," said Wayne, "you have to go for it when it's there. You never know what's going to be around tomorrow. Besides, Lisa's been talking up the idea of us buying a houseboat. The damn thing isn't cheap."

"She really keeps you on your toes, doesn't she?" I said.

"High maintenance," said Wayne.

"Oh, by the way, I saw her yesterday when she was going to the beach, and I'm afraid I spilled the beans about the fishing trip on Monday. I didn't know that she didn't know anything about it. Sorry."

"Oh well," said Wayne, "it looks like I'll be picking up a new piece of jewelry this weekend, then."

"Bribery?"

"Works every time," Wayne replied, smiling.

"So everything's going okay with you two?"

"Yeah, everything's fine," said Wayne, "I mean, I work a lot, and all, and she does her thing. But, as long as I keep bringing home the cash and a little trinket every now and then, things are cool. Unfortunately, this houseboat is a good bit more than a trinket."

"Yeah, I know," I said. "I saw it yesterday down at Gateway Marina when I was picking up bait. It looked like you could play a football game on it."

"So how have things been going with you guys?" asked Wayne. "Hey, Harry, any post-mortems from the leap into your truck?"

"No biggie," said Harry, "just a few bumps and bruises. Check this out, though." With that, he stood up, pulled up his shirt, and exposed his massive girth. "I got a nice one there on my back. See?"

"I was thinking we might have to call the fire department to get you out," said Wayne. "But you better be courteous and pull your shirt down now,

Harry. The people on the other side of the bar are eating."

"Very funny," said Harry.

"How about you, El?" said Wayne.

"Oh, same ol', same ol'. You know, I just keep slowly destroying the bodies of beachgoers on this island. They may have to declare my cart a Superfund site before long."

"What are you talking about, Ellis?" said Harry. "I never met a hot dog or sausage I didn't like. They're great."

"Well, that's good," I said. "It's people like you that keep my multimillion-dollar operation afloat. I may go public and start selling stock. How about Toxic Foods, Inc., the bane of a healthy Florida, initial public offering at $50 a share."

"Count me in," said Harry.

I saw Roger Carson settle up on his tab and walk around the bar toward us. "Goodnight, gentlemen," he said as he walked by. "In your case, Harry, I use that term loosely."

"This music too much for you?" asked Harry.

"No, I've got to go home and get my beauty sleep," replied Roger, "but I guess, Harry, you wouldn't know about that."

"Oh, funny boy," said Harry as he imitated throwing a punch by pounding his right fist into his open left hand.

"The boat leaves the dock at 6:00 a.m. Monday morning," said Roger. "Don't you boys be late or I'll be leaving without you."

"I'll be on time," said Wayne. "It's never a problem getting up early to go have fun."

Overhearing from behind the bar, Tom said, "Captain Roger, I shall see to it that Sir Ellis and Dr. Harry arrive in a timely fashion. I will be chauffeuring them to your vessel at the appointed hour."

"Okay, see you fellas Monday," said Roger as he turned and left the bar.

"Tommy, how about another round for us," said Wayne. "It looks like the band is about ready to start."

"Here, Tom, I got it," I said pointing to my cash sitting on the bar. "It's my turn."

It seemed a little incongruous that I would be buying Wayne a drink. He could buy and sell me a hundred times over, but this type of rotation was one of the unwritten rules of bar drinking. No doubt, Harry would pay for the next round.

"Thanks, Ellis," said Wayne.

"Yeah, thanks, El," said Harry.

Lil' Luther and Attitude Blue were back on the stage, huddled together. It looked like they were going over the songs for the second set. Tom leaned over the bar and spoke to the three of us, "Nothing against the blues, but I believe that jazz is a bit more cerebral."

Harry perked up and said, "Man, I've got your cerebral right here."

"No, Harry," said Wayne, "your problem is you've got your two cerebrals ass backwards."

We all laughed heartily. All of us except Harry, who said, "Oh yeah? I ought to give you the back of my hand."

"All right," I said, "everybody calm down. They're getting ready to play."

I had just spoken the words when the band tore into Stevie Ray Vaughan's "Pride and Joy." Lil' Luther was on. Like Stevie Ray, Luther could play both the lead and rhythm guitar parts at the same time. The regular guitar player in the band was strictly along for the ride. Unlike most blues songs that lament the negative aspects of love and relationships, the lyrics of "Pride and Joy" praised the singer's lady and virtually boasted of his love for her with the lines, "She's my sweet little thing; she's my pride and joy/She's my sweet little baby; I'm her little lover boy." I leaned over to Wayne during the guitar solo and said, "This is your song for Lisa, buddy."

Wayne nodded.

The crowd loved Luther's rendition. Stevie Ray Vaughan was widely popular and the patrons were clearly familiar with "Pride and Joy." It was a song the Texas-bred blues guitarist had successfully crossed over into mainstream rock.

It was incredible how Luther displayed such a wide range of talent. He played old and new, slow songs and fast. He cruised through blues by B.B. King, Robert Cray, Buddy Guy, and Muddy Waters. I got the impression the rest of the band didn't even know some of the songs. The drummer just kept a steady beat and the bass player followed along with standard chord changes the best he could. It didn't seem to make any difference because Lil' Luther was carrying the rest of them.

At one point in between songs, I leaned over to Wayne and said, "This kid's too good for this place. He could make it in Memphis or Chicago. Anywhere."

"You got that right," said Wayne. "I wonder where he's from and what he's doing here."

"Well, I intend to find out after this set," I said. "We better enjoy it while we can, because I'll bet he won't be playing around here for very long."

As Luther announced he was going to do a medley of Sonny Boy Williamson songs, Tom leaned over to us and said, "I do believe that Sonny Boy was considered a virtuoso on the blues harp."

"Tommy, get us another round on me," said Harry, "and what the hell's a virtuoso?"

"A virtuoso," replied Tom, "is defined as a person having great technical skill in the performance of music, my good man."

"Who the hell are you," said Harry, "Daniel freaking Webster?"

"I believe you mean Noah Webster," said Tom, "and no, I'm not. But I have read his dictionary."

"Hold that drink for me, Tommy," said Wayne. "I have to go in a few minutes."

We all listened intently to the music with an uncommon concentration. It sure wasn't a show you would hear every day at the Blue Moon. Really, any day at the Blue Moon. Luther had our attention. Before long, Wayne stood up and collected his money from the bar. After leaving Tom a sizeable tip, he said, "I've got to get going guys. See you Monday morning."

"Take care, Wayne," I said.

"Later, Wayne," said Harry.

Lil' Luther had blended together three Sonny Boy Williamson songs, "Low Down Ways," "Whiskey Headed Blues," and was just into the first verse of "My Baby I've Been Your Slave" as Wayne was leaving. The lyrics of that song woefully questioned how long the singer would have to endure the laborious bondage his woman maintained upon him, to the point of considering death as a means of relief. I turned and noticed Wayne hesitate at the doorway, listening.

When the song ended, I looked for Wayne again, but he was gone. Luther and the band finished the set with "Lonesome," which had been done by Memphis Slim. Luther sailed through an awesome guitar riff in the middle of the song. He was playing like there was no tomorrow. When the band finished the set and put their instruments down to take a break, I turned to Harry and said, "I'm outta here, but I have to talk to that kid for a minute."

Harry said, "Yeah, I'm later, too. I'll walk out with you."

We both left Tom a few bucks tip and said our goodbyes. I saw Lil' Luther go out the rear door of the Blue Moon, which led down a few steps to the beach. The rest of the band went to a nearby table and a pitcher of beer was delivered to them. Harry and I went around the bar and out the back.

A light breeze was drifting in from over the Gulf. There were a few lights from the back of the Blue Moon dimly illuminating a nearby area of the beach. When we got down to the sand, I didn't see anyone for a second. Then I noticed Luther in the shadows next to a palm tree. He was taking a smoke break. Harry could be a pretty intimidating form coming toward you in near darkness, so I called Luther by name as we approached. I wanted to put him at ease and let him know we meant no harm.

"Yes sir?" Luther replied.

"I have to tell you," I said, "that you just played and sang some of the finest music I've ever heard."

"Thank you very much, sir," said Luther, "I try my best."

"I'd buy you a beer, but I'm not sure you're old enough to have one."

"No, I'm afraid not," said Luther, "I'm only nineteen."

"Where did you ever learn to play the guitar and blues harp like that?"

"I've been working at it since I was ten years old," said Luther. "I live up in Gainesville, but I'm staying with my aunt in St. George for a couple of weeks. I heard they played blues at this bar and I thought I might be able to hook up with a band while I was down here."

"I've got to say you're head and shoulders above those other guys when it comes to playing the blues. You really ought to try to get with a more professional outfit. You've got the talent."

"Thank you," said Luther. "What do you think I ought to do?"

"Well, I don't know if you would want to try to handle the craziness of Chicago quite yet, but I really think you could make your mark in Memphis without any problem. You could walk up and down Beale Street and get a gig anywhere. They've got one blues joint right after another."

"Thanks for your suggestion," said Luther, "but I'm just kind of a Florida homeboy. I've never been out of the state."

"I'm telling you, with your ability, you could make it anywhere. You shouldn't fritter away your skills playing dives like this place. Don't waste your gift."

"I appreciate what you've said, sir. I'll think about it."

"In the meantime," I said, "I intend to listen to your music as much as possible while you're here. It's a real treat."

"Thanks again," said Luther as we shook hands. "I'll be here with the band next Tuesday."

Harry stepped over, shook Luther's hand and said, "Keep it up pal, you can really play."

Luther called thanks once more to us as Harry and I walked away. When we got around to the parking lot, Harry said, "There's nothing wrong with encouraging the kid, but you sounded like a parent or a teacher back there."

"I meant what I said."

"Yeah, but that stuff about wasting ability could apply to lots of people for different reasons," said Harry. "I mean, look at us, and Tommy, too."

We said goodbye and got into our vehicles. As I drove home, I thought about what Harry had said.

Saturday morning I was up and about early. Weekends were my busiest days for business at the cart. I did make time to go for a short run on the beach. There's nothing like breaking a sweat to make the body feel better after a night of beer drinking. Looking out over the crystal blue of the Gulf during the run made the mind feel better, too.

The pelicans were into their morning feeding session. They would glide along just a few feet above the water and then rise up maybe twenty or so feet in the air. Then, after a hesitation that seemed to defy gravity, they would cock their wings in an odd w-shape and dive straight down into the water

with a huge splash. It had the appearance of an unco-
ordinated, sacrificial kamikaze attack. But there was
method to their madness. After surfacing, they would
raise their head skyward and the lump of a whole
fish could be seen sliding down their gullet. As many
times as I have watched that maneuver, with great
fascination, I don't ever recall seeing a pelican come
up empty. It's really something to see. A much more
efficient technique than baiting a hook and waiting.

I jogged back to the house and got organized
for the day. I have a couple of citrus trees in my yard
that keep me supplied with oranges and grapefruit.
It's hard to beat a freshly picked grapefruit for breakfast. One of the simple pleasures of living in paradise. I also fired down a granola bar and a banana for
good measure. I made it a point to never skip some
form of breakfast. Most important meal of the day,
right?

I made my way up to the beach access and
set up my cart. I put out several large plastic containers that were marked for recycling. I encouraged my
customers to place cans, bottles, and plastic containers in the appropriate tubs. I would put the tubs in my
van at the end of each day and then periodically take
them to the county recycle bins. With the growing
number of people on the island and the refuse they
produce, recycling has got to be the answer. Without
being vigilant about recycling, we'll end up with a
landfill the size of a high-rise condo in no time.

Just as I was ready for business, a pack of
eight or ten senior citizens descended on my cart. A
morning walk on the beach was a regularly sched-

uled event for this group who lived on St. George Beach year-round. There were a fairly equal number of men and women. They came in all shapes and sizes, but the consistent trait among them was their lighthearted nature. If you couldn't have some fun and share a few laughs with this crowd, there was something wrong with you.

I hailed them as they approached. "Top of the morning to you, folks."

"Good morning," they replied almost in unison.

"What's the good word today?" I asked.

One of the ringleaders of this jovial band was a tall, thin man with jet-black hair. He was a Walter Matthau look-alike. "Well, the local chapter of the Florida Gray Panthers was just discussing the benefits of the season having ended. With the snowbirds back up north now, it gives us permanent residents a little more elbowroom around here."

"That it does," I said.

"Of course," he said, "you probably don't care for the drop in business with them gone."

"Oh, I don't know," I said, "we all can use a break from the crowds. I don't really mind. Besides, they'll be back before you know it."

"They certainly will," he said, "and next year they'll probably bring all their friends and relatives with them. I guess we can't gripe too much, though. We were all snowbirds once, ourselves."

"I know what you mean," I said, "most everybody on the island is from someplace else. There are very few true natives."

The seniors took their time, with everyone getting a little mid-morning snack. They bought bagels, donuts, fruit, coffee, iced tea, and spring water. They each had their favorites. Whenever they stopped by the cart, my business for the day always got off to a good start, both financially and socially. After about fifteen minutes of huddling in a circle filled with jokes and laughter, they went, as a unit, across the street to the parking lot and their cars. They were so cute.

Even with the season being over, I remained steadily busy all day. The temperature made it to the mid-eighties and there were only a few wispy passing clouds. The nice weather drew a lot of weekend day-trippers from up in St. George. The locals, however, differed from vacationers. The people that just drove over for a day at the beach were generally not big spenders. They would usually have sandwiches, sodas, and beer already packed in their coolers. They would occasionally buy from me, but not in large quantities. On the other hand, folks on the island for vacation didn't bother to make the extra preparations and, anyway, they were all set to spend some money. When you're in my business, you notice these things.

A little after four, I closed up the cart and brought my van over from its regular parking spot. On Saturdays, I had a different deal with the lot attendant. When I was done for the day, I'd haul the cart back across the street and park it and the van for a couple of extra hours in exchange for an Italian sausage, a bag of chips, and a soda. This was after the hot dogs I had given the fellow for lunch, which was our established agreement for free parking. I was slowly killing the guy, but he loved it. Crossing the Boulevard in my van with the cart attached wasn't too hard during the off-season, but it was a real trick during the busy winter months. At those times, it was forget finesse and just go ahead and bully. That was the only way to get it done.

My standard Saturday-after-work thing was to walk up to the nearby Shangri-La Resort on the beach. It's a seven-story hotel that is the epicenter of action on St. George Beach. During spring break, college students would seem to have the whole structure literally rocking back and forth. The place is informal to say the least. One side of the hotel has a tiny swimming pool. I've seen the water in that pool in more shades of green than you could shake a stick at. Not your crystal-clear bathing environment. More like someplace you could grow penicillin. On the beach side, there's a stage and an outdoor Tiki bar. Tables and benches run the entire length of the building with a direct view of the Gulf. Music plays continually, be it live or recorded. Both day and night, there is always a bustle of activity. During the day, the beach is a quagmire of partying humanity. Burly, beer-drinking guys in bathing suits intermingle with bevies of scantily clad girls. Thongs have been popular in recent years. It is *the* place to people watch.

Over the years, I had become acquainted with Tony Magdalene. Tony was the entertainment guru of the Shangri-La. He wore many hats, which included master of ceremonies, disc jockey, singer and impersonator. Tony was in his mid-to-late forties, with dark hair and tanned skin. He might as well have had the map of Italy tattooed across his face. He had been at the Shangri-La for as long as I could remember. We had a common background in that we both had grown up near Philadelphia. Occasionally, we talked about places on the Jersey shore that were familiar to each of us. Tony was a piece of work. He was skating his way through life with the best job he could have ever imagined. He was king of his domain, and his domain was paradise.

As I walked past the stage on the way to the Tiki bar, I caught Tony's eye. He was spinning records while the reggae band was on break. "How have things been going here at the asylum today?" I asked.

He gave me a thumbs up, and said, "The natives are restless, but I think I've got them somewhat under control, for now."

"That's why I'm only staying for a little while," I said as I walked off.

I took a stool at the Tiki bar and ordered a beer. Suspended from the ceiling of the thatched roof were televisions showing various sporting events. As if you needed additional stimuli to supplement the sideshow at the bar and on the beach. The vast display of skin, both standing around and on the move, was enough to arouse the most basic human instincts. Let me tell you, it was great. However, my long-standing practice of "look but don't touch," prevailed. I had never been much of a pickup kind of guy. I really had to get to know a girl before things would work the way they were supposed to. It was just as well I couldn't or wouldn't force it with a stranger. Occasional attempts in the past had yielded very disappointing results. Whenever I compared the modest benefits of casual sex with the effort required for a closer relationship, I viewed them both as a waste of time. With Marie, though, it was different. In a way, we were wasting each other's time. That sort of made it even.

I made conversation with a couple of the employees I knew, over the high volume of the music and the din of offshore jet skis. Stinking jet skis. I can't stand them. Beside the fact of the noise, air, and water pollution, I just plain don't get it. I would think you couldn't help but get sick of riding the damn things in about thirty seconds. I've got to say, their monotonous drone really had a way of taking the edge off the serene and natural setting of the beach. And their exhaust smelled the place up. What was that new term for them? Oh, personal watercraft. Personal watercraft, my ass. Half the people riding them didn't know what the heck they were doing anyway. If you want to be sporty and get some exercise, go for a swim for crying out loud. Ah, but they were good for the economy, I guess. That's what's important. Get people to spend their money at any cost. To hell with the environment. Let the next generation worry about it. Stinking jet skis. I guess I shouldn't hold back. I ought to tell you what I *really* think about them.

At around six o'clock, I settled up with the bartender and walked back past where Tony was conducting a limbo contest on the beach. Earlier, he had performed a couple of songs and had interviewed people on the beach with his mobile microphone. He had even graced the crowd with his long-dormant Elvis Presley impersonation. I hadn't seen him do that one for quite a while. His get-up was complete with a tight-fitting gold-and-white jumpsuit, black pompadour wig, and aluminum foil rings. Tony did his work, if you could call it that, with a vigor and enthusiasm that boggled the mind. It was like every day was his first day on the job. You had to admire the guy for his effort.

It would have been easy to sit there at the Shangri-La each Saturday until well past sunset and drink myself into a haze. That wasn't my style. Long ago, I had decided that Saturday was not the night for me to be out and about. Some of the craziest things on this earth happen on Saturday night and I've never wanted to be part of them. Call me boring, but that's

just the way I feel about the subject. Besides, Sunday would probably be a busy day at the vendor cart anyway. I was better off going home and sitting on my patio. Even if there weren't any fish jumping in the canal, watching the egrets and blue herons patrol the back yards until dark would provide me with enough entertainment.

The next day, customers kept me well occupied until mid-afternoon. After the season wound down, business tended to tail off earlier on Sundays. The more-local crowd left the beach and made their way home sooner than the winter residents did. Most of the locals had to go to work on Monday. I closed up a little before four, then drove back to the house and dropped off the cart.

Very few of my grandparents' friends on the island were still alive, but there was one couple, the Rosenbergs, who lived down the street from me. I had continued to have contact with them after my grandmother died. Irv and Mildred Rosenberg were so cool. They were both in their mid-eighties and, though moving a bit slower, they each were still very spry.

Almost every Sunday after work I'd go over to their house and visit with them. During the season, we would either barbeque or Mildred would make a casserole for dinner. Restaurants and takeout places were out of the question with all the mobs of people. When things quieted down, we would go out to eat for special occasions, but we all normally preferred to stay at their house. I had called them in the morning and let them know, on this Sunday, I would pick up Chinese food. I felt better when I brought something from time to time for us to eat, so Mildred wouldn't have to go to any special effort. I was convinced, however, she enjoyed making the preparations.

After picking up the Chinese food, I parked the van in my driveway and walked down the street to their house. As I approached, I noticed Mr. Rosenberg looking over some palm fronds that had fallen onto his side yard. I had known these folks since before I was a teenager and I still thought of them as Mr. and Mrs., but for years they had insisted on having me call them by their first names. For them, I think it put us more on an even level of friendship. Less formality. To please them, it was something I did, although I had never been very comfortable with it.

"Looks like you have some yard waste to deal with there, Irv," I said.

"And this is not all of it," said Mr. Rosenberg. "There's more in the back yard. I think the wind last night brought them down."

"Well, how about if we let it go for now and I'll round things up after we eat. I brought some Chinese food that's raring to go."

"Okay, then," said Irv. "There's not too much of it anyway. I don't want you to go to any trouble."

Mildred and Irv almost always had a short list of household tasks they would ask me to give them a hand with when I visited. They made a big deal, though, of not wanting to burden me with their chores. Actually, I didn't mind at all. I fixed up things for them I usually never got around to at my house. It made me feel good to help them out. They had someone who regularly cut their grass, and they employed a weekly house-cleaning service, but there were always other things around their place that needed some minor attention. I enjoyed being their part-time handyman.

As Irv and I walked into the house, Mildred hurried out of the kitchen to greet me with a big hug. "Oh, Ellis, how nice it is to see you," she said, standing up on her tiptoes to reach me. She had always been petite, but the advancing years had reduced her height even further.

"Mildred, it's good to see you, too," I said. "How's the lady of the house doing today?"

"Oh," she said, "one day at a time, you know. But I'm not complaining."

"Ellis, can I offer you a cold drink?" said Irv. "I just made up a yellow bird punch. You know, that's the one I say brings good luck."

"That would be great," I said.

The yellow bird consisted of rum mixed with a number of different fruit juices. Irv had a recipe, but he liked to improvise depending on what ingredients he had on hand. It was important to keep track of how many you drank, because the taste was so refreshing, it was easy to forget about the rum. They went down very smoothly. The custom of having a cocktail and relaxing before dinner was always the same with the Rosenbergs, but I found it humorous that they never failed to ask first. They were kind of formal in that way. I had the impression they rarely had a cocktail, except in these social situations. I think they really looked forward to it.

"Millie," said Irv, "why don't you put the Chinese food in the oven to keep it warm and we'll sit for a while and talk with Ellis."

I carried a tray with our drinks, and a few nibbles Mildred had put together, out of the back sliding glass door and onto their screened lanai. We could have been going to have a twenty-course meal, but Mildred would still have a few hors d'oeuvres prepared. It was a ritual with them. Their house was neat as a pin and it gave you the impression you were walking through a model home. The place was so spotless you could have eaten off the floor. They lived at the end of the street, and the canal behind their house opened up into Calusa Bay. The view from their lanai was beautiful. We toasted our glasses of punch and said, "Cheers."

With a little twist of his head, Irv said, "So how was business at your vendor cart today?"

"Things have calmed down some, recently," I said.

"I guess that's to be expected," he said. "The snowbirds have gone back north."

Mildred straightened up in her chair and said, "Did you meet any nice girls since the last time you were here?" She loved to play Cupid.

"No," I said, "you're just about the only nice girl I know."

"Oh, Ellis," she said, feigning embarrassment.

"Now, while I'm here I want to give you a hand with anything you need done around the house."

"We do have a couple of bulbs out in the track lighting, said Mildred, "and Irving has a few things out in the yard, but it's really not very much. We don't want you to go to any bother."

"No bother at all, Mildred. After we eat I'll take care of it."

"That's so nice of you, Ellis," she said.

"Oh, Irv," I said, "I'm going out on a little fishing trip tomorrow. If I get any decent-sized grouper, I'll bring you some."

"Grouper would be nice," said Irv.

After a bit, we brought the Chinese food out to the lanai and sat at their glass-top table. As we passed the containers around and filled our plates, I said, "I kept my fortune from the last time we had Chinese food. I taped it up on my refrigerator. I don't know if you recall, but it said, 'Nature, time and patience are the three great physicians.'"

"That was a good one," said Irv.

"Ellis," said Mildred, "we went to the matinee at the dog track on Wednesday. It was the first we had gone since December."

"Oh," said Irv, "we had a grand time."

"I think you two have the right idea by not going when all the crowds are here," I said. "The traffic is terrible, and with the way people drive, you have to be very careful."

"You're not going to believe what happened," said Mildred. "Irving, you tell Ellis the story."

"In the fourth race," said Irv, "was this dog named Delaware Pride. He was a long shot, ten to one. Well, as you know, we're from Delaware, Ohio. Just a little north of Columbus. So, we had to bet on this dog. I gave Millie ten dollars and she put it all to win on Delaware Pride. You know what? The dog won the race. It paid $22.80 on a two-dollar bet, so we cashed our ticket for $114.00. How about them apples?"

"That's great," I said. "It sounds like you both had a very successful outing. You know, it's kind of a coincidence about the name Delaware. Where I grew up in Pennsylvania, we lived only about fifteen or twenty minutes from the State of Delaware."

"Well, how about that," said Mildred. Then after a short pause she asked, "Any news from your family back home, Ellis?"

"Well, I haven't been up there in a long time," I said, hesitating. "You know I'm not very close to my parents. I don't think they have ever accepted my way of life. I didn't follow in the family footsteps and become a pharmacist. Although we don't talk much, I do know my father has been getting some routine treatments for cancer recently. But neither one of my parents has made a big deal about it."

The three of us then ate quietly until Irv leaned toward me and said, "So Ellis, you tell us what's new with you."

"Oh, just keeping busy every day with the cart, you know." Then straightening in my chair, I said, "Irv, there is something that's been on my mind lately. Maybe you can help me with it."

"I'll do the best I can," he replied, raising his index finger, "but remember—my consultation fee ain't cheap."

I gave a little laugh and then said, "Well, in dealing with people I know, it seems like I keep facing these issues of working and making money and ambition and happiness and—"

"Whoa, hold on there a minute, Ellis," said Irv. "One thing at a time."

"But that's the whole problem for me," I said. "It's all of those things tied up together. I mean, you look at somebody who has the ability to be really good at something, to be a success in a certain field, and what if that person's not excited about that. Maybe they'd rather do something else to be happy. Maybe that something else doesn't earn them as much money or have as much status or prestige. What's right and what's wrong in that situation? What do you think?"

"Let me put it this way," said Irv, "and this is not a criticism of your generation. But for those of us who lived through the Depression, we just didn't have the luxury of making those kinds of choices. You worked wherever you could and tried to make as much money as you could. Hunger can be a big motivator. In my case, I was lucky. Back in Ohio, my father and uncle owned a small grocery store together, so that's where I worked. There wasn't really any other thing to do as far as I was concerned. When they retired, it became my store and for the past twenty years it's been our son's store. That's just the way things went. You didn't give it much thought."

"But what about happiness?" I said. "Doesn't that mean anything?"

"Happiness?" said Irv. "You were happy if there was food on the table and a few bucks in the bank. That was happiness. You did what was needed to get by. There weren't any better alternatives. But enough of my Depression-era spiel. That might not have anything to do with what you're talking about."

"I don't know, Irv," I said. "I guess I get confused when I see what people do or don't do with their lives. When I look at what drives them or what doesn't drive them, I get stumped."

"Well, Ellis, life itself is confusing," said Irv. "Sometimes there is no explaining people's behavior. I guess there are different things that motivate different people. Many times, I think people make their decisions based on the way they feel at the present. What seems right to them at that place in time. If they do that, then down the road they can't be too critical of those earlier decisions. There may not be much point in trying to figure it all out. Look, I don't know if I'm even addressing exactly what you're hung up about. I'm sorry if I don't have the answer for you. Maybe you're just asking the wrong guy."

We finished eating and I went about the house taking care of a few things for the Rosenbergs. As it was getting dark, we said our goodbyes. I walked up the street, went past my house, and continued across the Boulevard. I walked out on the beach and looked over the Gulf. There was no breeze at all and there wasn't a sound to be heard on the sand. What I could see of the water was calm and still. It seemed more like a big lake. A crescent-shaped new moon sat low in the western sky. It took on the appearance of a bowl sitting upright, as if it could hold water. When I was a kid, I'd always heard that meant it wasn't going to rain. Just to the right of the moon, the planets of Mars and Venus were aligned in a unique arrangement. Their bright, off-white colors set them apart from the stars that twinkled in the dark sky. I stood and stared at the interesting trio for ten or fifteen minutes. Then I turned and walked home. Since I was going fishing the next day, I decided to go to bed early.

# 11

As the first hint of morning light peeked through the window of my living room, I walked out the front door and went around to the garage. I noticed a thick, almost sweet, pungent odor from the night's dew that had settled on the yard. In the garage, I got my fishing equipment together. Promptly at 5:30, Tom Grissom pulled into the driveway and we proceeded to load my gear in the back of his pickup truck. He had a cap covering the bed, which kept things dry when it rained.

"Good morning, my dear sir," said Tom.

"How are you doing, Tommy?" I asked.

"I'm doing okay," said Tom, "but for the hours I normally keep, this is still the middle of the night."

"I know what you mean. I rarely get up this early myself. It gives you a whole different outlook on the day."

Tom had picked up three large Styrofoam cups of coffee, and I sipped on one as we drove up the Boulevard toward Harry's house. When we arrived, Tom hopped out of the truck and went to the front door. I got out and stretched. I heard Tom ask Harry if he could use the bathroom. Harry replied, "Yeah, man, no problem. Just don't make too much noise, Brenda's still asleep."

After Harry loaded his fishing equipment and Tom returned, we piled into the pickup. I got in the middle, and as we drove away I felt like I was cramping Tom's ability to drive. We were shoulder to shoulder, due to the fact that Harry took up about half of the truck's bench seat.

"You're not getting any smaller on us now are you, Harry?" I said.

"No way," said Harry. "It takes a big hammer to drive a big nail, you know."

"My good man," said Tom, "you certainly have a way with words."

"Yeah, Harry," I said, "don't waste all of your humor on us. Save a little for Wayne and Roger. We don't want them to feel left out."

"No problem," said Harry. "I've got plenty."

"That's what we're afraid of," said Tom.

We arrived at Roger's boat, the Lady EC, a little before six. Roger had named the boat after his wife's initials. Her name was Eleanor Carson. Roger was kidded occasionally that EC was a popular nickname for the well-known musician, Eric Clapton. Not being a student of music or performers, Roger didn't get the comparison. He didn't know who Eric Clapton was.

Wayne was already there and was helping Roger check some of his supplies. Roger had been running fishing charters out of St. George Beach for over thirty years. More recently, he had wound down his business to just occasional half-day trips for friends and acquaintances. However, Roger still spent much of his idle time around the North End Marina. He continued to be a prominent figure in the fishing community and was looked up to as a mentor by the younger charter boat captains. It was said of Roger that he had forgotten more about fishing in Southwest Florida than many other area watermen would ever know. When it came to fishing lore on St. George Beach, Roger was widely recognized as the ultimate source of wisdom.

"Morning, gentlemen," said Roger as we brought our gear onto his boat, "and you too, Harry."

"Ha, ha," said Harry with a sarcastic manner. Then in a serious tone added, "Now, Roger, are you sure you have enough coolers on this boat to hold all the grouper I'm planning on catching today?"

"Yeah, I think we're all set, Moby Dick," said Roger. "Welcome aboard."

We settled in as Roger slowly directed his boat out of the marina. Fishing, both sport and commercial, was big business around St. George Beach. Boats of all shapes and sizes packed every available slip at the marinas that dotted the island. Their variety ranged from small sloops—some housing seafaring vagrants who had chucked it all—to luxurious yachts, to battle worn crafts of professional shrimpers and fishermen. As we eased our way toward North End Pass, we went by an old barnacle-encrusted trawler that was tied to the dock. Out of a door to the interior quarters of the trawler emerged a hard-as-nails woman in a ratty, pink chenille bathrobe. Following close on her heels was a mangy-looking cat whose apparent purpose was to patrol the fishing boat for unwanted varmints. Here at our island paradise there certainly exists a wide range of lifestyles.

As we exited the Pass and went into the Gulf, Roger increased the speed of the boat. Our Captain planned to go out about twenty-five or thirty miles and set us up in an area he believed would produce some nice-sized grouper. Tom joined Roger up on the bridge for the trip, and Harry kicked back on a padded bench, pulling his cap down over his face. I snugged up the leather straps of my plantation owner's hat to make sure I didn't lose it off of my head and into the Gulf. Wayne sat next to me at the stern and, with the engines roaring at high throttle right behind us, we could just barely hear each other.

"How was your weekend, partner?" I asked.

"Oh, pretty good, I guess," said Wayne. He turned his head and looked out over the sparkling water as we streaked ahead on a smooth course. After a few minutes, he turned back and said, "You know, Ellis, I've been thinking about things since I saw you at the bar the other night."

"What kind of things?"

"Well, about Lisa and me and our marriage. You asked me if things were going okay," he said, turning his head away, and then after a pause he turned back and said, "and I'm not so sure anymore. It seems like our whole relationship is based on money. It has gotten to the point where we don't ask each other how we are, or how we feel anymore. It's more like, she always wants to have an update on how much money I'm making, and I'm asking her to show me the latest thing she bought. Man, when we were dating, we'd make up a picnic lunch and go down to the state park and just talk the afternoon away. Then sometimes at night we'd drive down to the beach and walk and watch the stars for hours. We never do anything like that anymore. It's like neither of us want to make the effort. Now, we always involve another couple or a group of friends. When it's just the two of us, we'll go a long time not talking at all, and when we do, it's either about things we own or things we want to buy. I don't know what the answer is."

"Look, Wayne," I said, "I'm no marriage counselor. I'd like to say something very insightful and have it be the magical cure for you, but I have a pretty bad track record when it comes to dealing with women. The one thing I've always heard, and it seems like pretty good advice to me, is finding a common ground or having a common interest is the place to start."

"In a way, that's just the thing," said Wayne. "In the early going for us, it seemed like we were both equally interested in making a life together by acquiring money and possessions. I think we both thought by doing that, we would find happiness. Well, we've done a whole lot toward that end, but it hasn't resulted in your so-called marital bliss. I mean, I make all this money and we own all these things, but I really can't say we're happy in the classic sense. We kind of just exist together, in wealth."

"I don't know, my friend," I said. "You hear that money can't buy happiness, and maybe it's true, but I hope you two can work things out." I hesitated for a second, and then added, "If that's what you want, Wayne. I'm in your corner no matter how things go."

"Thanks, Ellis," said Wayne. "I sure do want it to work. I still love her, damn it."

After heading west into the Gulf for a little over an hour, Roger cut back the engines and the boat slowed to a halt. Without dropping anchor, Roger busied himself by helping us all get set up. He had made sure we had everything we would need, from bait, to beer, to box lunches. We all had given him an appropriate share of money to cover the expenses of the trip, with an additional sum to be kept by him for his efforts. Harry baited his hook and dropped it overboard well before the rest of us. After only a matter of seconds had passed, he had a bite.

"Yeah, man," hollered Harry, as he pulled a big, beautiful grouper on board. "Ring the dinner bell, baby. Whoa!"

Throughout the morning Roger moved about the boat, assisting us in every possible way. We each caught a few keeper grouper. Harry, however, made it clear to everyone that he was having the best day. For him, competitiveness was a big part of the fishing experience. After landing what was easily the largest fish up to that point, Harry called out, "Yo, Roger, you're going to have to come over here and give me a hand. My arms are getting tired pulling in all these fish."

Roger walked over close to Harry and said just loud enough for the rest of us to hear, "You act like an asshole, and you don't get invited back."

"Right," said Harry, as he baited his hook and turned away.

And then, one of the funniest incidents in recent memory happened. Instead of dropping the baited hook over the side of the boat, Harry reached back to set up a dramatic cast of his line. As his arms wheeled the rod forward with a surge, he let out a scream that could have been heard for miles. He had hooked himself in his right buttock. All hell broke loose on the boat. Wayne and I were able to exchange high fives before being stricken with out-of-control laughter. I was having trouble breathing. Roger managed to get out, "Oh man, I hate when that happens."

Tom, who had been fishing toward the front of the boat, on the opposite side, came back to see what all the commotion was about. Just as he came around the bridge with his rod in hand and realized what Harry had done, Tom got a hit on his line. As he broke into hysterics, the rod was jerked away from him and into the water. Between bouts of laughter, Tom got out, "Now that's a situation."

Wayne's face was scarlet from laughing when he hollered, "Harry, it looks like you've got a personal problem."

All the while, Harry was stomping around and yelling, "Come on guys, you've got to get it out of there. Ow, man, Ow!"

With each additional cry for aid, the rest of us burst into a higher crescendo of laughter. I barely had enough air to say, "That's a real character builder there, Harry."

Harry continued asking for help by pleading, "Man, this really hurts, get it out."

Finally, Roger got himself calmed down enough to try and remove the hook. Several times he approached Harry's rear end with a pair of pliers, only to have a wave of laughter come over him and foil the attempt. Harry yelled on, "Oh, man, Roger, get that goddamned hook out of there."

Wayne again chimed in, saying, "It's all over but the shouting, boys."

When Roger finally removed the hook and held it in the pliers for all of us to see, he said, "Now ain't that a revoltin' development." Roger then went below and brought back the first-aid kit. To see him applying antiseptic cream and bandages to Harry's rear end did nothing to reduce our laughter. Although he was hurting, we really worked Harry over. We weren't going to miss a chance to bust on him after all the bragging we had put up with earlier.

Wayne put on a straight face for a second and said, "Have you had a tetanus shot recently, Harry?"

With a nasty look, Harry shot back, "What do you think? In my line of work, of course I have."

The self-inflicted wound pretty much put an end to any further fishing. We all had gotten some nice grouper, so we ate the box lunches Roger had provided and drank a few beers. Captain Roger had iced tea. On the way back in, Harry laid on the same bench he had used on the morning voyage, but on this trip he was face down on his stomach to keep weight off of his injured butt cheek. Several times during our return, one of us would point at Harry's large form that engulfed the cushions of the bench, and the laughter would start up again.

When we arrived back to the North End Marina, the beers and the bouncing ride had taken its toll. All of us except Captain Roger had to relieve ourselves, big time. The four of us scrambled off of the boat and went around on the decking to the backside of the bait shop, which was protected from public view. As if on cue, four streams hit the water below at the same time.

"Oh, baby," said Wayne, "does that feel better."

"Yeah," I said, "I feel like a hundred bucks."

We finished up and paraded back around to Roger's boat. While we were gone, our good Captain had unloaded the coolers that held our catch of grouper. He'd placed them next to the cleaning table on the dock. We set up a makeshift assembly line and proceeded to scale and clean the fish. Layering with ice, we then packed the grouper back into our various coolers. During the operation, a group of pelicans, eager for a handout, sat in the water below and disposed of all the refuse that was dropped to them. Seagulls circled the area, but they knew better than to interfere very much with the pelicans. When it came to a pecking order between seagulls and pelicans, pelicans rule, hands down. The gulls were lucky to get anything.

When the cleaning project was completed, Wayne suggested we go down to the Blue Moon for a couple of beers. Roger declined the invitation. He saw a group of charter boat captains talking outside the bait shop and decided to join them. As we carried our tackle and coolers to the parking lot, we heard Roger call out to his other buddies, "Wait 'til I tell you about the best catch of the day, fellas." Wayne, Tom, and I broke up laughing yet again. Harry kept on walking and showed no reaction.

Tom drove his pickup with Harry on board and I rode with Wayne in his BMW. It was late in the afternoon as we went into the Blue Moon, but the sun was still shining brightly. We were greeted by Lydia, the owner, who was behind the bar. When Tom was off, Lydia filled in as barmaid. She was short, heavyset, and had a tough appearance. In the Blue Moon, what she said went. If someone started acting up when she was around, she'd be all over the perpetrator in a heartbeat. With her reputation as an enforcer, there was rarely any trouble, at least with the regulars who knew her style. Although Lydia took crap from no one, she had a heart of gold, particularly with people she knew well. Based on her outward behavior, you never would have known she was an old softy toward those she cared about.

"Well, well," she called, "you leave the door open and there's no telling what might wander in."

"I assume that's you, Lydia," I said, "but give me a minute to let my eyes adjust to the light to make sure."

"Oh, it's me all right," she said, "which makes it your lucky day."

Wayne placed a twenty-dollar bill on the bar and said, "You better start us out with a pitcher, Lydia, we got awful thirsty on that five-minute drive from the marina."

"So how did you boys make out on your little fishing trip today?" she said. "I want a full report."

"Let's put it this way," Wayne said, laughing, "the rest of us will be sitting down, but I'm afraid Harry's going to be standing."

"What's this all about, Harry?" she asked, setting the pitcher of beer on the bar.

Before Harry had a chance to answer, Tom broke in, "Well boss, you see, Dr. Harry here had a bit of a mishap earlier. With an ill-advised cast from

Captain Roger's vessel, he managed to land a hook into his right gluteus maximus."

"That's good," said Wayne, "gluteus maximus. Does that make him a glutton for punishment?"

"In this instance," said Tom, "I believe it does, indeed."

"That's a real shame, Harry," said Lydia, smiling. "I hope you've had your tetanus shot."

"Yes," said Harry, in a stern voice, "I've had my goddamn tetanus shot."

Tom raised the palm of his hand and said, "Don't be offended, boss, by Harry's acidic demeanor. He was asked that same question a bit earlier. And whenever our dear Harry sinks a fish hook into his posterior, he tends to become a bit testy."

Lydia waited until our glasses were filled, then placed a zippered plastic bag full of ice cubes into the remaining beer in the pitcher, saying, "This pitcher's on me, fellas."

After we all thanked her, Harry said, to no one in particular, "Don't worry, I'll be fine in a couple of days."

"I'm not sure there's enough days left in the year to really make you officially fine," said Wayne.

Before Harry could respond, I decided to change the subject to keep things calmed down, "You know, Tommy, it's kind of strange to see you on this side of the bar."

"I have to admit," said Tom, "it gives you a whole different perspective on things. Although it's probably best it doesn't happen very often." Then to

Lydia, "By the way, boss, I don't think we will require the bag of ice to keep the remaining beer cold. It will no doubt be gone shortly." Tommy then turned to me and said loud enough for Lydia to hear, "If I don't keep an eye on her, she wastes bar supplies at every turn. I hate to imagine what goes on here when I'm not around."

With the early morning start we'd had, along with the boat ride, the sun, and the laughter, not to mention the numerous beers, it didn't take too long for things to deteriorate into a drunkfest. Because Monday was a slow day, and there were very few other patrons, Lydia was patient with the four of us. The final straw, however, was a couple of hours later when Harry went to take a drink and missed his mouth completely. Beer spilled down his shirt and onto the floor.

"Looks like there must be a hole in the old lip there, Harry," I said.

Wayne leaned over and said, "Well how about that. Now you've got one to go with the hole in your ass."

At that point, Lydia decided to call a halt to the proceedings and suggested we all go home. Wayne came up with the brilliant idea of calling a cab. In fact, he called for two cabs—one to take him to his place up in St. George and one to take Tom, Harry and me down the island to our houses. We settled up with Lydia, the best we could manage, and when the cabs arrived, we staggered down the front steps. Wayne went around to the driver of our cab and handed him some money. He leaned in the window and said, "Boys, the ride home is on me. You know, Harry, you may not be able to work tomorrow with your little impairment there."

"No problem, Wayne," said Harry, "I never call out of work. I'll go in, believe me. Even if I have to take a pillow with me."

# 12

I felt pretty hollow the next morning, even though I had gotten home fairly early in the evening and had gotten a full night's sleep. Since I didn't take off from work very often, it was unusual for me to have been involved in an all-day drinking binge. I walked down to the beach and did my best to get in a short run. It was more like a slow trot, but I managed to get a sweat going and I felt a little better when it was finished. Going for a swim was completely out of the question. I knew I wouldn't drown if I stayed on the beach. As I walked back toward my house, I saw Tom Grissom's pickup parked in my driveway. He was sitting behind the wheel, reading the newspaper and drinking a cup of coffee. He looked sort of like death warmed over.

"Hey there, Tommy," I said as I approached his truck. "And how might you be feeling today?"

"To be straightforward," he said, "I basically feel like shit. I'm not used to a drinking session anything quite like that. I'm more accustomed to watching other people get drunk while I serve them."

"Yeah, that was a lot for me, too."

"I have arrived with your fishing equipment and your cooler of grouper," said Tom. "I rode my bike up to the Blue Moon a little while ago and retrieved my pickup. I checked on the fish and there's still some ice left in the coolers. The grouper are fine. If you don't mind, can you keep Harry's stuff too? I went by his house, but he'd already gone to work."

"Sure thing, Tommy," I said, "I have plenty of refrigerator space in the garage."

We unloaded everything from his truck and Tom drove off, looking pale as a ghost. I froze most of the grouper but set aside four nice filets to take to the Rosenbergs. I gave them a call, and then carried the fish down to their house on my bike. They were delighted.

"Thank you so much," they said together. When they got excited, they often spoke at the same time.

"That'll make a couple of nice dinners for you two," I said.

They thanked me again, and Irv said, "Now you get going off to work, Ellis." Then gesturing with his index finger, "Don't keep those customers waiting."

I went back home and rinsed off. Not even sure if it was a full-fledged shower. I still wasn't thinking very clearly. It was quite an effort to hook the cart to my van and drive up Calusa Boulevard. I struggled through the first few hours and really didn't start to feel better until early afternoon.

A little before four o'clock, as I was getting ready to close up for the day, I was startled by the loud blast of a truck horn. It was Harry, driving his company's tractor and flatbed trailer, which was carrying a chained-down forklift. He had stopped in the middle of the Boulevard. He yelled to me, "Ellis, meet me over at the Shangri-La in a half an hour."

"Are you kidding me?" I called. "I had enough of that yesterday."

"I'm telling you," Harry hollered, "I gotta talk to you. I'm going to park this rig back at the nursery and get my pickup. Meet me at the Shangri-La in a half an hour. It's important."

"Okay, okay," I yelled, "half an hour."

Cars became stacked up behind Harry's trailer and the drivers began to honk impatiently. As he started to pull away, Harry responded by honking the air horn again and thrusting his left hand out of the window of the cab with his middle finger raised. I shook my head as the semi, blowing billows of black exhaust, moved slowly and loudly up the street. I kept the cart open for fifteen or twenty minutes and then locked it up. Since I didn't intend to stay at the Shangri-La for very long, I didn't bother to bring my van over and make the crisscross of the Boulevard as I did after work on Saturdays. Whatever was so important that Harry wanted to talk about had better be brief, I thought.

As I walked around to the beach side of the Shangri-La, I heard Tony Magdalene before I saw him. He was doing impromptu interviews on the beach, which always started out with the question, "Where are you from?" On this day, Tony was easy to pick out because he happened to be wearing a white lab coat. He had his portable microphone in hand and was milling through the group of beachgoers who remained from the day's sunning. Tony was also promoting the happy hour shooter of the day that waitresses were carrying around on their trays. The shooters were contained in small test tubes and were bright green in color. A shade of green not unlike one I had seen before in the Shangri-La swimming pool. The whole scene looked like some kind of whacked-out chemistry experiment. I guess, in a way, that's what it was, with Tony playing the role of the mad scientist. For him, it was just another day at the office.

I walked over to the Tiki bar and ordered a beer. I knew the first one was going to be kind of rough to get through. I had to chew it down. When I had almost finished it, and was starting to feel better, I saw Harry walking toward the bar from the far end of the Shangri-La. When he caught my eye, he stopped and waved for me to follow him. I paid for the beer and walked between tables, in Harry's direction. I saw him sit down on a bench beyond the end of the large awning, which shaded much of the ground level on the back of the hotel. On my way, I stopped a waitress who was wearing a bikini top and a white mini skirt. The material of the skirt was so thin, the thong underwear she was wearing was clearly visible. I didn't know what the skirt was made of, but it was so sheer you could have read the newspaper through it. She wasn't the prettiest girl, but her figure and the outfit were impressive.

"Would you bring my buddy and me a couple of beers, please," I said. Then pointing, "We'll be sitting on the bench down at the end, where the sun is shining."

As I approached, Harry was looking out over the Gulf. His eyes had a distant blank stare that told me he didn't even see the people on the beach. That was unusual, because ordinarily when Harry came to the Shangri-La, he would intently survey the crowd for attractive-looking girls. It was one of his favorite pastimes. I figured something was up.

"Okay, big guy," I said, "what the hell's going on? I wasn't planning on coming here after work today and I wasn't planning on drinking beer today either. Is there a goddamn crisis or what? And what's with all the secrecy, sitting way down here?"

"There's a goddamn crisis, all right," said Harry. Then after a pause, "Oh, man."

"Well, what is it?"

"There's no way to ease into this, so I'm just going to say it. Lisa is cheating on Wayne."

"What?" I said. "Are you nuts or are you on some kind of medication?"

"You heard me," he said. "I saw it today."

"Saw what?" I said. "And start from the beginning. You've got to be kidding."

"No kidding, Ellis," said Harry. "Okay, here goes. I was working with my crew down in Malaga today. They're just about finished the new library, and we were working on the landscaping, putting in palm trees and shrubbery on the property."

Abruptly, Harry stopped talking. The waitress was delivering our beers. She set them down and said, "Do you want me to run a tab, guys?"

"Yeah," I said, "I think that would be a good idea. This might take a while."

After the waitress walked away, Harry continued, "So, anyway, right before lunch, I was backing the flatbed across the street and into the parking lot of the Holiday Inn. I was going to turn it around in their lot, which is huge. I'm watching the ass end of the flatbed out of my big side mirror and I see Lisa McMillan getting out of her Jag that was parked on the side of the motel. There was a black Lincoln parked next to her with a guy sitting in it. He was dressed up with a jacket and tie on. She leans in the window and gives the guy a kiss."

I interrupted, "You're seeing this with the side mirror of your truck?"

"Now wait a minute," said Harry, "let me tell you the whole story."

"All right, all right," I said, "go on. I'm riveted."

"So I back the rig all the way past where they're parked, to the back of the lot. The guy, who looked like he was maybe sixty, gray hair, very distinguished, gets out of the Lincoln, and the two of them walk up the stairs to the second floor. While the guy is unlocking the door to one of the rooms, Lisa stands at the railing and looks back and forth over the parking lot. Then she turns and walks into the motel room and closes the door."

"And she doesn't see you in the tractor?"

"Look," said Harry, "there's a lot of construction going on down there in the newer part of Malaga. Heavy equipment is all over the place. I don't think she was looking for me, if you know what I mean. No, she didn't see me sitting in the tractor, okay?"

"I don't believe I'm having this conversation. Are you sure that fishhook in the butt yesterday didn't give you some weird strain of yellow fever or something? Are you sure you're seeing straight or do you have a case of double vision?"

"Dammit, let me tell you what happened."

"Go on, go on," I said, rolling my eyes.

"I parked the rig and turned the engine off. I walked across the street to my crew and told them to take their lunch break. Then I went over to the Eckerd drugstore and I bought one of those little disposable cameras. It takes like six pictures."

"Oh, boy."

"I went back to the Holiday Inn parking lot," said Harry, "and I took a picture of the back of the cars, Lisa's Jag and the Lincoln. I'm sure I got the license plates."

"I'm sitting here talking to Sherlock Holmes."

"Then I walked between a parked car and this stockade fence that hides the garbage dumpsters. I stood behind the fence and waited."

"Garbage dumpsters," I said. "How did it smell back there?"

"I'm going to finish the story whether you like it or not," said Harry. "I watched the door of the room like a hawk and a little less than an hour later it opened. I snapped a shot of them just stepping out of the room, and one with them on the walkway of the second floor. Then I got a picture of them halfway down the steps while they were holding hands. The next shot he's holding the door for her to get into her car, and in the last one he's leaning in the window and giving her a kiss. What do you think about that?"

"I think you're missing out on a career as a soap opera writer."

"I'm telling you the truth, El," said Harry. "It happened."

We stopped talking as our waitress approached and asked if we wanted another beer. I nodded and said, "Yeah, two more would be great." When she left, I turned to Harry and said, "Hey, I'm not calling you a liar. I just think maybe you have a vivid imagination. Maybe it was somebody else. Are you sure it was Lisa?"

"Sure as shit," said Harry.

"Okay, so where are the pictures?"

"I took the camera back to Eckerd's," he said. "You have to give them the whole thing with the disposable kind. They develop the pictures overnight. I can pick them up tomorrow after two o'clock. We're still going to be working down at the library."

"Well, I don't know, Harry. This is a little tough to swallow."

"Look, Ellis, would I bullshit you about something like this?"

"How soon do I have to answer?"

"I'm telling you what I saw," said Harry, "and tomorrow I'll have the pictures to prove it. Now listen, Ellis, there's something else."

"What now?"

"I've got to tell Wayne," he said. "I've thought it over and I don't have any other choice. We've been friends our whole lives. I couldn't ever look him in the eye again if I keep this from him. I'm going to call him tomorrow and tell him to meet me at the Blue Moon when he's done work. I'd like you to be there, too."

"Count me out," I said. "I have no intention of getting involved in any of this, Harry. It's your baby."

"Come on, Ellis, I could really use you being there. Besides, Wayne likes you and trusts you."

As our waitress delivered our beers, I said to her, "I think that will do us. We'll take our check, please."

She totaled up the tab and set it between us. I reached out and grabbed it to keep Harry from getting his hands on it. After she walked away I said to Harry, "I'm not getting in the middle of this. It's none of my business. If you're so sure about it, then you do what you have to do."

"I figured I could count on you to help," said Harry.

"The answer is no," I said. With that, Harry got up without touching his full beer and stormed off.

I sat on the bench for a while, sipped on my beer, and looked out over the Gulf. I pulled some cash out of my pocket and unfolded the check that had been crumpled in my hand. At the top of it, I saw how the waitress had noted where we were sitting. I half laughed to myself as I read: IN SUN DOWN FAR.

# 13

After I went home and took care of some overdue paperwork, I decided to go up to the Blue Moon and catch a set of Lil' Luther and Attitude Blue. It had occurred to me earlier in the day they would be playing, but the way I had been feeling made it unlikely I would go. After the couple of beers at the Shangri-La, I felt much better. Also, I needed some kind of distraction to get my mind off of what Harry had told me. I was kind of dazed by the whole thing, even though I still had serious doubts about the validity of what he claimed to have seen. With Harry's reputation of twisting facts and embellishing stories, I wasn't convinced the story was true. It was sort of like not believing the boy who cried wolf.

I made some dinner, showered, and drove up to the Blue Moon. As I got out of the van and walked across the parking lot, I saw a large German shepherd standing near the pay phone on the side of the building. The shepherd was peering around the corner and looking up toward the front door. When I got closer, I noticed the dog's leash was tied to the receiver of the phone, which was off the hook. Apparently, the dog's master was in the bar. I figured there was little chance anyone would try to make a call with Rin Tin Tin attached to the phone. I gave a wide berth to the shepherd as I walked toward the front steps. The unusual behavior of some of the customers of the Blue Moon never ceased to amaze me. I went in and saw Tom was at his regular post behind the bar.

"Hey, Tommy," I said as I pulled up a stool. "What's with the guard dog outside?"

"I beg your pardon?" he said. "What guard dog might you be referring to?"

"Somebody has their German shepherd tied up to the receiver of the pay phone outside."

Tom laughed and said, "Well, I trust you stayed a prudent distance away from someone's idea of a canine patrol."

"As a matter of fact, I did," I said. "I don't think that phone's going to get much use for a while. By the way, you look a hell of a lot better than you did this morning."

"Thank you," said Tom. "And, indeed, I do feel a hell of a lot better. Am I correct in assuming you are here to listen to your precocious, guitar-playing prodigy?"

"You got it," I said. "For most of today, though, I didn't think I was up to it. But I'm feeling better and I thought I might listen to a set or two.

Anyway, I needed to get my mind off some things Harry was telling me a little while ago. You never know when to believe him and when not to believe him."

"Well," said Tom, "it is certainly true that Mr. Forte does have the proclivity to misrepresent the facts upon occasion."

"I don't feel like getting into it right now," I said, "but this time I think Harry may have gone off the deep end."

"Oh, my," said Tom, as he walked away to get someone a drink.

The members of Attitude Blue began bringing in their equipment and setting up for the evening. As I watched them working up on the stage, I heard a voice behind me say, "Good evening, sir." I turned to see it was Lil' Luther, holding his guitar case and spreading a broad smile. He was dressed in the same suit and tie he had been wearing the first night I saw him, but everything about him looked fresh and pressed.

"Hey there, Luther," I said, "how's it going?"

"Just fine, sir," he replied. "I want to thank you again for what you told me the other night. I've been giving it some thought."

"Look," I said, "I'm not trying to tell you what to do, but I think you really have the talent to move up and make it with a better brand of musicians. No offense to the rest of the band here tonight."

"I talked to my aunt about it," said Luther, "and she was pretty reluctant at first. But I do think I've made some progress with her, though. She called my mother up in Gainesville and they chatted about it. I don't think either of them want to hold me back."

"Well, you keep at it," I said, "and somebody in the music business will discover you, if you know what I mean. You play in the right places and it's bound to happen."

"Thanks again," he said as he walked over to the stage.

In a short time, the band was ready to play. They started out with an instrumental I didn't recognize. It seemed like a warm-up number. The group had a tighter sound than before, giving me the impression they had rehearsed together since the first night I heard them play. Lil' Luther introduced the next song, "Have You Ever Been in Love" by Sonny Boy Williamson. It was interesting to see that Luther was now doing the announcing. I guess the rest of the band had accepted the fact they had hooked up with a rising star and they were going to ride with him for as long as possible. Lil' Luther sang and played the blues harp with energy and emotion. The way he wailed the song, expressing such legitimate sadness, you might have thought that a woman he deeply loved had left him earlier in the day. When it came to making the lyrics seem convincing, Luther gave it his all.

Toward the end of the song, I turned and noticed Harry had taken the stool next to me. I hadn't received the usual forceful physical greeting he was accustomed to giving. He just sat there and waved Tom over when the music stopped.

"Beer, Tommy," he said. Harry was giving me his version of the cold shoulder. He finally turned to me and merely said, "Hey."

I nodded my head, and with a gesture of my thumb toward the stage said, "Our guy is back playing again and the band is letting him do the intros."

"They're using their heads," said Harry. "Luther is better than anybody those other guys will ever get a chance to play with."

Tom drew Harry a beer and set it in front of him, saying, "Good evening, Mr. Forte. I trust you are on the mend from yesterday's ill-fated accident, and that an amputation of your posterior will not be necessary."

"Real funny, Tommy," said Harry. "Don't you worry your pretty little head about it. I'll be fine."

"That is encouraging news, my friend," said Tom. "Do keep me posted on your recovery. However, I would prefer the reports be infrequent and with very little detail."

"Right," said Harry. "By the way, Tommy, when you get a break with the customers, there's something I'd like to talk to you about."

Tom nodded as he walked away. I looked at Harry, shook my head, and said, "How many people are you going to involve in this, buddy?"

"Look," said Harry, "it's just you and Tommy. I didn't make much progress with you, so I'm going to pour my heart out to my favorite bartender. That's what he's here for, right? It's part of his job."

"Yeah, that's what they say."

After a minute, Tom came back to us and said, "Alright then, Harry, the bartender of this venerable saloon can spare a few minutes, but I might urge you to give me a condensed version. I am gainfully employed, as you know, and I wouldn't want your fellow patrons to be kept waiting."

Harry proceeded to fill Tom in on the same story I had heard earlier. Tom was attentive until Harry had finished.

"Your story," said Tom, "is very interesting. However, there are several points I would care to make. Number one, the still photographs you have mentioned will provide credibility to your observation. Even so, they will be a far cry from having moving pictures with sound."

"Cut the bullshit, Tommy," said Harry, "and admit that I have got to tell Wayne."

"Number two," said Tom, holding up two fingers, "by taking into account your lengthy friendship and the gravity of the situation, I concur with the need to communicate your findings to Wayne. I do believe, however, that by making him privy to the details of your account, as well as to the evidence, you will tend to emasculate him."

"Look," said Harry, "I'm not freeing any slaves here."

"No, no my friend, that would be emancipate," said Tom. "Emasculate means you may weaken or destroy his strength and vigor. In other words, he will be hurt tremendously."

"I know that, Tommy," said Harry, "but I can't let him go on thinking Lisa is faithful to him when she isn't. It would hurt him way more to find out later that I knew about it and then didn't say anything. He'd feel like even more of a fool."

"I do believe you are correct on that score," said Tom, as he left us to wait on other customers of the Blue Moon.

"Harry," I said, "this is some serious shit you're talking about here. There isn't any room for error. You better have it right, because you could come out of this looking like a real asshole. You've got to be sure."

Harry looked me straight in the eye and said, "I've never been more sure of anything in my life."

During our conversation, the band had been making a few technical adjustments. When they were completed, Luther offered a compelling version of the mournful Elmore James classic, "The Sky Is Crying." The song told the gloomy and dispirited tale of the singer's love for his mate that he suspects has gone unrequited. With the lines, "I'm wadin' in tears lookin' for my baby/and I wonder where can she be?" Elmore James told it all. It can't get much bluer than that. Lil' Luther sang with such emotion that the listener was left to imagine that only a heavy rainstorm could be comparable to the volume of tears that he had shed.

Man, oh, man, Luther was good. He had the ability to tailor his style from one song to another by adapting to the original artist's performance and interpretation of the music. There was a soulful depth in his voice and an amazing dexterity in his playing of the guitar and blues harp. He capped the whole thing off with a passionate presentation. And it was all wrapped up in a nineteen-year-old body. Unbelievable.

At the end of the first set, I felt a wave of fatigue come over me. I turned to Harry and said, "I'm beat, my friend. I'm going to hit it. Oh, I have your grouper from the fishing trip that Tommy dropped off this morning. I marked it for you and put it in the big chest freezer in my garage. Come and get it anytime you want. You know where the key is."

"Thanks, El. I'll swing by in the next couple of days. It's not going anywhere. I think I'm gonna stay for one more, then I'm outta here, too. What do you say about tomorrow night? I could really use you being here when I talk to Wayne and give him the pictures."

"No go, Harry," I said. "I have my regular date with Marie on Wednesday night, but even if I didn't, I wouldn't want to get in this mess."

"Okay, I'll do it myself," said Harry, with a miffed tone of voice. "No thanks to you."

I settled up with Tom and, as I stood to leave, gave Lil' Luther a thumbs up and a wave. I turned, patted Harry on the back a couple of times, and left.

# 14

On Wednesday, business at the cart followed the regular routine. The group of seniors, out for their walk, came by and got my commercial enterprise off to a good start, as usual. I never ceased to be impressed by their jovial, upbeat nature. The positive attitude they maintained was practically universal among them. Occasionally, if one in the group was not in a good mood or began complaining about something, the balance of the pack would kid and cajole the dissenter. Almost always, he or she would quickly be coaxed back into the fold. Their viewpoint on life had a way of making me unconcerned about the prospect of old age. They made it seem fun. Maybe it was because, at least as it appeared, they had their physical health. Perhaps, in turn, that contributed to their mental health. Regardless, I enjoyed their company and took pleasure in seeing them each day they came by. I was enamored with them far beyond their profitable impact on my business. Without any specific effort on their part, they would never fail to leave me with a smile on my face and with an uplifted mood.

Off and on during the day my thoughts drifted back to Harry's story about Lisa McMillan. My frame of mind was at its worst when there were gaps of time between customers. I still was not convinced Harry had actually seen what he claimed. Even though Wayne had confided to me on the fishing trip that his marriage had weakened somewhat, I just couldn't see why Lisa would jeopardize her lavish lifestyle. I didn't see what there was to gain from her standpoint. Lisa and Wayne seemed to have it all. They were both still in their twenties. They were both good-looking. They had plenty of money. All of that made you figure they had a bright future. Well, at least financially. It made me wonder, what more could anyone want? Of course, I had never been married or ever had a lot of money. What the heck did I know? I peddled hot dogs out of a vendor cart. That sure didn't make me any kind of an authority on the subject.

I went home after work and relaxed on my back patio. For a while, I distracted myself by watching for mullet leaping out of the canal. I also think the little lizards, known as geckos, that scurry about the stones and pavers are very interesting. They're about four inches long and very thin. Those lizards are very quick on their feet and they're everywhere in Southwest Florida. I'd get a kick out of watching their interesting rituals, which sort of resemble play. One would chase another and then they both would stop and do what appeared to be a series of fast push-ups. Whether it was a form of intimidation or a love dance, I didn't know. I'm no biologist. In any event, their behavior was intriguing to me.

I showered and put on one of my few tropical shirts I reserved for occasional wear on date night. I figured it was okay to look a little touristy every now and then. I wore standard jean shorts. Clean ones. I wasn't going to cave in completely to fashion with some trendy linen slacks or something. I had to draw the line somewhere with the dressy thing. A little before seven, I walked up to Marie's apartment. She looked great, as usual. She had on a white blouse and a black pair of shorts. The blouse against her dark skin made for a stunning contrast. The thought went through my head that I was a pretty lucky guy to be hanging out with Marie.

We followed our standard path over to the beach. There were times we were together when there would be large gaps in our conversation. It didn't seem to bother Marie and it surely wasn't a problem with me. I believed we were just comfortable with our companionship. We didn't press anything. That was especially true when we walked on the beach. We would stroll along and take in the beauty of the sand and the Gulf. Sometimes we'd stop and look for attractive shells that had washed up on the beach. Different types of birds also drew our attention. We'd see small sandpipers huddled in a group and, when the water receded from the beach, the little guys would race forward and sink their beaks into the sand all at the same time. Then they'd retreat just as quickly before the next incoming covering of water. They're quick enough to avoid getting anything but their tiny feet wet. Seagulls are not as industrious in finding food as other types of birds. Gulls are scavengers who depend either on handouts from humans or uneaten leftovers from other birds. I've even seen them try to perch on top of pelicans in the water, waiting, usually unsuccessfully, for possible discarded pieces of fish. I have never cared much for

seagulls, especially after I had heard them character-
ized as rats with wings when I was a kid.

Marie and I took our time walking up the
beach to the Beer Garden. When we arrived, Luis
greeted us with his usual enthusiasm. He seated us at
a table on the deck near to the outdoor bar. The urge
to talk about Harry's supposed discovery overcame
me and I said to Marie, "Are you ready for the latest
from Harry Forte?" Marie had met my friends from
the Blue Moon on a number of occasions and was
familiar with their various personalities from stories
I had told her.

"I'm not sure if I am," said Marie. "Should I
assume it's his standard line of bull?"

"Well, I don't know for certain yet," I said,
"but Harry claims to have seen Wayne McMillan's
wife, Lisa, yesterday down in Malaga at the Holiday
Inn."

"So?"

"He said Lisa was with some other guy and
the two of them spent the better part of an hour in one
of the motel rooms."

"Now that makes it more interesting."

"Yeah, Harry said he took some pictures that
will prove his story."

"Wow," said Marie, "I'd say he's going to need
them for anybody to believe this one. I mean, what
would Lisa McMillan be running around for? Why
would she take a chance on losing what she's got?"

"I thought the same thing, but Wayne did tell
me the other day he and Lisa weren't quite as tight as
they used to be."

"If I were her," said Marie, "I'd make that marriage work. Wayne's loaded."

"I don't know, Marie, if it was anybody but Harry telling the story I think I'd be more willing to believe it."

"Good point. So what's going to happen?"

"Harry has probably met with Wayne by now to tell him," I said. "He was supposed to pick up the pictures today and then see Wayne after work at the Blue Moon. Harry wanted me to be there, but I said no. I thought it should be between the two of them. They've been friends practically their whole lives."

"I think it's best to stay out of it," said Marie. "What if it turns out to be typical Harry bullshit? You don't need to get involved with that. I think you did the right thing."

"Thanks. Time will tell."

Both of us had ordered the blackened mahi-mahi and, when our plates arrived, it appeared we had made a good choice. Digging into the tender filets, we both nodded to each other in agreement. The fish was delicious. I had never had a bad meal at the Beer Garden and I'd never heard anybody else say they had either. As we ate, I noticed Marie was wearing a very pretty ring I had never seen before. The large, rectangular stone was pale blue, almost turquoise, in color and was translucent.

"Marie, tell me about the ring you're wearing. It's really nice. I've never seen it."

"My mother gave me this ring," she said. "I hardly ever wear it. It's a blue topaz and it came from Brazil. It was my grandmother's."

"Why don't you wear it more often?" I said. "It's beautiful. I don't think I've ever seen one like it."

"Oh, I'm always afraid something's going to happen to it," she said. "I wouldn't want to lose it or have someone steal it."

"Well, I don't agree with your thinking. If you have something very nice, like that ring, you should wear it and enjoy it. What good does it do just sitting in a drawer or a safe somewhere? If you never see it, it's like it *is* lost or stolen."

"I want Sandra to have it some day," said Marie. "I don't want to take too many chances with it."

"I can understand that to a degree, but life is short. I think that if you have nice things and then don't wear them or use them, you might leave this world regretting it."

"You may have a point, Ellis," said Marie, smiling. "I'll think about it."

While we were eating, I couldn't help but notice two men walk onto the deck and go to the bar not far from our table. I pointed them out to Marie. They appeared to be unlike the rest of the customers in an odd kind of way. Both of them were dressed in worn jeans and shabby shirts. One guy was a Sam Elliott, the actor, look-alike. His face was swarthy and thin, but handsome. He had graying hair sticking out from beneath a baseball cap and he had a large gray mustache. The other guy looked like an anorexic Willie Nelson. He had long, scraggly hair and his face was scruffy with whiskers. The burnt-out hippie type. In the Blue Moon you would never have given those guys a second thought. They would have blended right in with their looks and the way they were dressed. The Beer Garden, however, was a nice restaurant so they seemed to stand out.

At the bar, they greeted two other men who were already seated. The way they were introducing themselves and shaking hands, it was apparent the pairs were not very familiar with each other. The two that had been sitting at the bar had a completely different look than the rough guys. They appeared to be in their mid-twenties, were clean-cut, and nicely dressed. The four of them had a beer and talked. The Willie Nelson guy had a lot of nervous energy. He was constantly fidgeting and had outbursts of loud talking. He acted like he might have been on some kind of drugs. If he was, it was definitely something stronger than marijuana. Without finishing their beers, and with their tabs still on the bar, the foursome left. I leaned over to Marie and said, "I think we just might be seeing a drug deal in progress."

"Something sure seems odd about all of that," said Marie.

After about ten minutes, the four returned and finished their beers. They talked for a little bit and then the rough-looking characters left. The remaining pair ordered another beer and, when it was served, they toasted each other. I looked at Marie and said, "I do believe we've pegged what's going on."

Before we finished our meal, the two younger guys at the bar paid their tab and left. Luis stopped at our table as we were getting up to leave and talked with us briefly. We said goodbye and walked down off of the deck and around the restaurant. As we turned to cut through the parking lot, we saw two police cruisers sitting next to the side of the building. An officer from the sheriff's department was standing near the clean-cut guys who had, only minutes earlier, left the Beer Garden. The two of them were sitting on a bench and they did not look very happy at all. A second cop was sitting in his cruiser talking on the radio. As we walked past the scene and then onto the beach, I said to Marie, "Well, I don't think that whole thing was what we thought at first. I think we had it backwards. I'll bet you the two rough-looking guys were undercover narcs. They probably just bought drugs from the two on the bench, and then had them busted."

"Nothing surprises me around here anymore," said Marie.

We walked down the beach and watched a colorful sunset. The weather forecast for the next day called for some morning rain. High clouds had begun to dot the sky and, as the sun lowered, brilliant shades of reds and pinks reflected off of them. We lingered on the beach until it was almost dark and then walked back to Marie's apartment.

# 15

As I was getting ready to leave Marie's place on Thursday morning, I noticed the sky over the Gulf of Mexico looked very threatening. I put on one of several tank tops I kept for casual wear around Marie's apartment, and rolled my folded tropical shirt in a plastic grocery bag. As I went down the outside wooden steps, I saw a dark, nasty curtain of clouds moving quickly toward the beach. The smell of impending rain was in the air so I broke into a jog. I figured I might be able to make it home before the bottom dropped out and, at the same time, get in my daily exercise. It sure wasn't going to be a morning for swimming in the Gulf. The wind was really kicking up, and when I was about a block and a half from home, it began to pour. There were sheets of big drops slanting in on a forty-five-degree angle. I hate going out to run when it's already raining, but if it starts coming down after I'm out there, then that's okay. There must be some weird jock mentality about that.

I was drenched to the bone by the time I reached my house. I peeled off my clothes and hopped into a warm shower. When I got dried off, I turned on the television and checked the marine weather channel. The radar showed a series of rain bands headed over St. George Beach. That set up what the weather people referred to as a training effect, which meant it would continue to rain over the same area for a substantial period of time. There would be no working today, I thought. Rain was one of the occupational hazards of my profession. Of course, the good part was that there were more rainy days in the summer months when it wasn't as busy anyway. Still, it seemed like just about the only time I was off was when it was raining. Unlike salaried folks, though, I didn't make any money when I wasn't working the cart. That was okay. I didn't have a boss either.

I spent the morning doing laundry and straightening up the house. I went out to the garage and took an inventory of my supplies for the cart. I wrote up a list of what was needed for my weekly order and put it on the kitchen counter. I'd make the standard call to my supplier in the early evening. Around ten-thirty the phone rang. It was Irv Rosenberg. "I knew you'd be home with this storm we're having," he said. "How about coming over for lunch? Mildred can make up some fish sandwiches with that grouper you brought us."

"Are you sure?" I said. "I thought you two could have a couple of dinners with those filets."

"Would I be calling you if I wasn't sure?" said Irv.

"Well, that sounds great. What time?"

"Noon would be good."

"I'll be there."

When I was getting ready to go to the Rosenbergs' house, the rain started to let up a little, so I just grabbed an umbrella and walked down the street. Mildred and Irv greeted me in their customary cheerful manner. "I hope you brought your appetite, Ellis," said Mildred as I entered.

"What's different today, though," said Irv, "is no cocktails and no list of chores. Just food and conversation."

"That's fine with me," I said.

You would have thought Mildred had anticipated the meal since the day before. She had made potato salad, coleslaw, and fresh fruit cocktail to go with perfectly broiled grouper sandwiches on sourdough rolls. Being the joker that he was, Irv quipped as we were starting to eat, "I bet you were expecting the fish to be on Jewish rye, already." What a card.

"Mildred, the lunch is delicious," I said between bites.

"What do you mean, Mildred?" said Irv. "I've been slaving over a hot stove all morning and you're thanking her."

I just laughed and winked at Mildred, knowing full well she was the chief cook of the house. When we finished eating, we relaxed and sipped on our iced tea that had fresh sprigs of spearmint poking out of the glasses. The Rosenbergs were great for seeing to every little detail in everything they did. They didn't know any other way.

"So, Ellis," said Irv, "what is on that mind of yours today?"

"Well," I began, "in a similar vein with what we talked about last Sunday, there's something that may have happened this week that has me even more mixed up about people and life. I don't want to get into specifics because I'm not sure if it's true, but why would someone risk a secure life with money and status just for a fling?"

"I'm not just sure exactly what you mean, Ellis," said Irv, "but there is an old saying that goes 'People only want what they cannot have.' Does that fit in with what you're getting at?"

"You may have something there, Irv," I said. "Some things just don't add up when it comes to people's behavior. Maybe I'm a perfect example of that. You know about my family background. My father and brother are both pharmacists and that's what I thought I wanted to be when I was younger. Instead, I dropped out of college, then moved down here and became a beach vendor. How do you figure that? You wouldn't think it makes sense."

"Now, Ellis," said Irv, "there's nothing wrong with what you do. You make enough money to support yourself. You don't have other responsibilities. You don't have a house full of kids looking at you and wondering where the next meal is coming from. Now that's pressure. Because you live by yourself, you have the luxury of running your life any way you want to. If you're happy, and I think you are, or ought to be, you shouldn't have any misgivings about your work. The world needs vendors like you. I bet that you like most of your customers and I guarantee your customers like you. A very rich man once defined success as finding a need and then fulfilling it. That's what you've done, Ellis. In your own way, you're a success."

"And besides," interjected Mildred, "we think you are a wonderful person."

"You know," I said, "you two seem to always have a way of making me feel better. Maybe I shouldn't try to figure everyone out, myself included. I guess I tend to overanalyze and take people's behavior a little too seriously."

By a little past one, the rain had stopped and the cloud cover was beginning to break up. I thanked the Rosenbergs profusely for the terrific lunch and we said goodbye. Mildred even gave me a covered bowl of the potato salad to take home. She mentioned that I could bring the bowl back on my regular visit on Sunday.

As I walked up the street, I negotiated around large puddles that had been created by the morning rain. It is a common occurrence for there to be ponding of water after a heavy storm on the relatively flat terrain of Southwest Florida. With the high water table and the vast amount of pavement, runoff and absorption is a slow process. In many cases, the water just doesn't have anywhere to go.

When I got home, I noticed there was a message on my answering machine. I hit the play button. It was Wayne McMillan. A chill shuddered through me as I listened. Wayne, in a very calm but very serious voice, asked if I would meet him at the Blue Moon around five o'clock. He said he wanted to talk to me in person. His voice was recognizable, but not his manner. I was worried. Maybe Harry Forte wasn't full of shit after all.

I sat for close to a half an hour in an absent-minded funk until I heard the sound of a vehicle in the driveway. It was Harry in his pickup. It occurred to me that the rain had kept him out of work, too. I was standing in the front doorway as he walked up.

"Come on in, big guy," I said. "What happened with Wayne last night?"

"Oh," said Harry, "so now you're interested? I thought you didn't want any part of this mess."

"Well, Wayne left me a message on my answering machine while I was down at the Rosenbergs' house for lunch. He said he wants to talk to me at the Blue Moon around five."

"Now isn't that a coincidence?" said Harry. "He just called me at home and said the same thing. I guess he figured we were both off today."

"So what did he sound like on the phone?"

"Pretty much just like he did last night when I showed him the pictures. His voice was kind of in a monotone. Plus, last night when he talked to me he had this faraway look in his eye. Afterward, Tommy said, with some of his fifty-cent words, that Wayne looked like he was suffering from a malaise that was akin to a form of dementia."

"Oh yeah?"

"Uh-huh," said Harry. "Tommy explained it as having a loss or impairment of mental powers."

"So the pictures are for real then?"

"Do you finally freaking believe me?" said Harry. "I've been telling you the truth all along."

"I'm sorry, Harry. I just couldn't see Lisa doing that."

"Yeah," said Harry, "you and me both. Anyway, Wayne didn't go wild or anything last night. He kept his composure during the whole conversation.

At the end, he put the pictures in his suit pocket and shook my hand. He even thanked me."

"Oh boy. That has got to be one tough situation to be in."

"Yeah," said Harry, "better him than me."

We sat and drank a couple of beers. Both of us were in a pretty subdued mood. The cat was really out of the bag and neither of us felt very good about it. Harry said he had a couple of errands to run and he would meet me at the Blue Moon at five. After he left, I listlessly finished my laundry. My head was somewhere else.

Since the nasty weather had cleared out, I decided to ride my bike up to the bar. My morning scamper in the rain hadn't really qualified as a workout so I thought a little pedaling was in order. Funny thing, I did a lot of bicycle pedaling and hot dog peddling. Anyway, I wasn't planning for it to be a long evening. I figured I'd be back well before dark. At twenty of five I headed up the Boulevard.

As I wheeled my bike into the parking lot of the Blue Moon, I saw Lisa McMillan's Jaguar convertible sitting right next to the building near the bicycle rack. I knew it was her car because I was familiar with her license plate, which was a vanity tag that read "My Toy." The old pulse went up a couple of ticks. What the hell is she doing here, I thought. I'd only seen her at the Blue Moon maybe a couple of times ever. I got this eerie feeling there might be some kind of showdown coming, which was not very comforting. The thought of leaving crossed my mind, but a strange curiosity gripped me. I decided to stay. I locked up my bike and walked around to the front.

As I went through the open doorway and my eyes adjusted to the dark interior, I saw that the place wasn't very crowded. There were four or five guys spread around the bar and an older couple was at a table in the corner. Lisa McMillan was sitting on a barstool with her back to the door. She had a glass of wine in front of her and she was wearing enough jewelry to sink a battleship. From behind the bar, Tom caught my eye and made a facial gesture that told me he didn't know what Lisa was doing there either. I had no choice but to pull up a stool beside her.

"Hey there, Lisa," I said, "what brings you to this ol' hole in the wall?"

She turned and with a manufactured smile said, "Oh, hi, Ellis, how are you doing? You know I don't come around here very often. It's really not my style. Wayne asked me to meet him here at five."

"Uh, good."

"I guess there was no hawking the old hot dogs today," she said, with a cynical feel to it. "The rain must have kept you indoors."

"Right," I replied. "Today was an administrative day."

Tom came over and greeted me saying, "Good day, sir, what will it be?"

"Draft please, Tommy."

"Now, Ellis," Lisa went on, "when are you ever going to get a real job?"

"You mean, so I can have a boss telling me what to do? Or so I can pay a whole bunch of taxes?"

"Yeah," she said, laughing, "something like that."

"I don't expect it will happen anytime soon."

By the way the conversation was going, it was obvious that Wayne had not confronted Lisa, and that unsettled me even further. Talk about feeling nervous. I hadn't noticed Harry Forte come in the bar behind me, so when he slapped me on the back and said, "What's happening, buddy?" I practically jumped through the roof.

Harry turned to Lisa and said, "Hey, good looking, what's going on?"

"Hi, Harry," said Lisa. "I bet you're another one who was off because of the rain. No palm trees got planted today, huh, big guy?"

"No," said Harry, "my crew got a break from me bossing them around today."

Harry sat down beside me and ordered a rum and coke from Tom. At that point, I was thinking some hard liquor would be a good idea for me, too. I was about to order a shot, which was a rarity for me, but I didn't get the chance. There was a loud screeching of tires coming from out in the street, and then a skidding sound in the crushed shell parking lot near the front door of the Blue Moon. Harry and I jumped up and darted to the front window. Wayne's white BMW had slid to a stop practically at the base of the front steps. He hopped out of the car and slammed the door. Wayne was dressed in a nice suit, as usual, but his tie was all crooked and the collar of his jacket was turned up. His hair was mussed and he was holding a half-empty bottle of Absolut vodka in his right hand. I had never seen him look that way before. He was a mess. With his left elbow tucked tight against the side of his suit jacket, he took a swig from the bottle and then slammed it down on the hood of the car. There was an intense, bitter look in his eyes as he yelled, "LISA!"

Harry, who was standing right next to me, muttered under his breath, "Holy shit."

Again Wayne yelled, "LISA!"

Lisa stood up and twice used her fingers to sweep her long blond hair back behind her ears, exposing humongous diamond earrings. She had a nervous smile on her face as she shot a glance toward Harry and me. I felt like my body was turned inside out. Wayne yelled for Lisa a third time as she stepped to the open doorway and said, "Wayne, what are you doing yelling like that? You're embarrassing me."

It was the oddest view to see Lisa standing in the foyer of the Blue Moon and to look through the window and see Wayne. They couldn't have been more than ten or twelve feet apart. Only the four brick steps separated them.

"Embarrassing you?" Wayne said. His voice was now controlled but firm. Although it was apparent he had been drinking, he didn't slur his words. His emotions were stronger than the alcohol. "I could tell you a thing or two about being embarrassed," he said.

"Wayne, what is this about?" said Lisa as she started to step out through the doorway.

"Stay right there you cheating bitch," said Wayne, holding the palm of his hand out as a stop sign. "I'd like you to tell me and my friends there in the bar what it's like to screw around on your husband."

"What are you talking about, Wayne?" said Lisa. "I don't know what you're talking about."

"Oh, really?" said Wayne. "Maybe these lovely eight-by-ten glossies will refresh your memory a little." From inside his jacket Wayne pulled out a large envelope. As he took out a handful of photo enlargements, the envelope fell to the ground and he said, "I had them blown up today so nobody would have any trouble recognizing you with your boyfriend." Slowly, Wayne peeled off the six pictures one by one while holding them out at arms length.

"Wayne," said Lisa, "let's go home. This is no place to be talking about this."

"Oh, I think it's the perfect place," said Wayne as he threw the photos at her and they landed scattered about at her feet. "Maybe you'll tell the truth here. Home is where we lie to each other. Right? Like when you tell me some bullshit story about what you do during the daytime. And then like last night when I told you I loved you when we were having sex."

"What?" said Lisa, stepping forward.

"I said stay there," said Wayne, as he pulled a pistol from his jacket pocket and pointed it at Lisa.

"What are you doing with a stupid gun?" said Lisa. "You don't even know how to use it."

"Stay right there," said Wayne, "or you'll find out I can use it."

Harry leaned close to me and whispered, "I've never seen him with a gun in my life."

"Yeah," said Wayne, "I told you I loved you, but I lied. I had to have you one last time. I had to. But I hate you now more than I ever loved you. Go ahead and say it. You've been cheating on me. Go ahead. Say it. SAY IT!"

"Okay," said Lisa, her voice breaking up, "I've been seeing someone else. Is that what you want from me? Is that what you want, Wayne?"

"Why, Lisa?" said Wayne, "Why? There's never been anything I wouldn't do for you. I've worked my ass off for you. This guy must have more money to spend on you. Is that it? More money? Is that what you're looking for? Is that what you want?"

"It's not the money, Wayne," pleaded Lisa, half crying. "It's not the money. I found someone who pays attention to me. Someone who wants to be with me and talk to me. You're never around. You're always working."

"Working to make money for you, Lisa."

"He pays attention to me," said Lisa.

"Oh, really?" said Wayne. "How about telling me and the boys in there how he pays attention to you. What positions does he like to get you into

121

when you're shacking up with him for a sweet little matinee at the Holiday Inn down in Malaga?"

Lisa regained her composure like the flip of a switch, and then with a wry smile said, "I screw his brains out."

"You fucking slut," said Wayne. The words were barely out of his mouth when he fired two quick shots that blasted through her chest, spurting blood out both her front and back—momentarily freezing her like a statue. In the split second while she was motionless, Wayne took sharper aim and fired one more shot that blew through her forehead. A gory spray of blood spewed out the back of her head as she was flung backwards against the foyer wall. She had to be dead before she hit the floor.

Wayne shoved the gun into his jacket pocket, grabbed the bottle of vodka and jumped into his car. Without thinking, but by mere reaction, I yelled to Tom to call 911. Wayne whipped the BMW around and flew out of the parking lot. His spinning rear tires rained crushed shells up the front steps and through the open doorway. The BMW's tires were wailing as the car rocketed south on Calusa Boulevard. Harry rushed over to check Lisa, but it was no use. Her lifeless body lay in an ever-growing pool of blood. I'd never seen anything remotely close to what had just happened and it shocked me into a stunned stupor. For a moment, I thought for sure I was going to throw up.

In what seemed like no time, the sound of sirens could be heard in the distance. A lot of them. Seconds later, sheriff's cruisers and rescue vehicles rolled up with lights flashing and sirens screaming. It looked like a scene from a movie. I went over to the bar and spoke in a low tone to Tom, "Look, Tommy, there are plenty of witnesses here. If the cops want anything from me, give them my phone number. I'm getting out of here. I'm going home."

"You got it, Ellis," said Tom.

I walked around the bar and, as I reached the back door, I turned to see paramedics and police swarming in the front. While the EMS team went about their business with Lisa, Harry immediately engaged the cops. Having lived on the island for years, and also being a veteran of more than a couple of altercations, Harry knew practically every member of the sheriff's department. I'd guess he knew at least half of them on a first-name basis. He was pointing back and forth and talking in a loud voice over the noise of the sirens outside. His demonstrative explanation certainly had the attention of the officers. Harry was holding court and, in his own way, I knew he loved it.

I went down the back steps to the beach and caught a quick glance of the peaceful waters of the Gulf. What a contrast it was to the gruesome carnage that had just transpired. As I turned the corner of the building and started to unlock my bike, I hesitated for a second in disbelief at the site of Lisa's Jag sitting there. She'll never drive that again, I thought. I walked my bike out to the sidewalk and took a last look at the assemblage of police cruisers and ambulances in front of the Blue Moon. Then I rode aimlessly back down the Boulevard.

# 17

I just plain didn't know what to make of Wayne's reaction. I figured he must have envisioned his whole world unraveling right before his eyes. He probably saw the fruits of all of his hard work going down the drain in a big way. To him, Lisa had always been the prize for his arduous labor. She had been not only a motivator for him to earn and succeed, but she was also the recipient of his efforts. She was an integral part of everything he did. Mainly due to her, Wayne had driven himself from an average middle-class guy to a wealthy young man. I imagined that dealing with her betrayal of him was too much for Wayne to handle. He was only twenty-eight and he still had the youthful fire of emotion burning in him. Something deep down inside had snapped and I figured Wayne probably couldn't envision things ever being the same again. What a shame.

I began to think of what the outcome would be for Wayne. How and when would he be arrested? Would he resist the police or would he turn himself in? Where had he gone? Where was he now? As I turned my bike off of Calusa Boulevard and onto my street, I quickly got the answer to a couple of my questions. In my driveway, about a hundred and fifty yards away, sat Wayne's white BMW. It looked like there was the profile of a person sitting behind the wheel, but from that distance I couldn't tell for sure. Instinctively, I brought my bike to a quick stop. Oh shit, I thought. What am I going to do now? Isn't this just great? There in my driveway sits a friend of mine who, only fifteen minutes ago, murdered his wife in broad daylight. And not only that, but he had proven both Lisa and Harry wrong about not knowing how to use a gun. What kind of luck is this? He's currently a felon on the lam that is very much wanted by the police and he picks me to visit. Excellent.

I wondered about his current frame of mind. Had he finished the bottle of vodka? Did he still have the gun? Was it still loaded? Why did he want to see me? Was he suicidal? If I talked to him and said the wrong thing, would he shoot me or maybe himself? My mind raced through numerous scenarios in a millisecond. I took the easy way out. I turned my bike around and continued riding south on the Boulevard. Had he seen me? Did he want me to help him turn himself in? Why the hell was this happening to me? Is this the price of friendship? I kept asking myself questions that I didn't have answers for. All I knew was I had no desire to become any more involved in the ongoing soap opera. Boy, in the movies, people do these heroic acts. A character says the right words and saves the day. It occurred to me, in real life, things don't necessarily turn out that way. In real life, you blurt out a line someone doesn't like and you end up like Lisa McMillan. I enjoyed living a little bit too much to take a chance that might happen to me. Let somebody else be the hero for this one.

I reached the south end of the island and parked my bike at the foot of the bridge over Gateway Pass. I locked it to the same pole I always did when I fished there. Then I walked up to the middle of the bridge, leaned on the railing and looked out over the Pass, which opens into the Gulf of Mexico. That sight had always been very comforting to me, but now it soothed me to a far lesser degree. The beauty of the view was wasted on my agitated state of mind. I looked around and saw some familiar faces of fishermen on both sides of the bridge. As usual, there was very little conversation going on. People were just fishing and minding their own business. A little small talk here and there. One angler on the Bay side of the bridge hooked a good-sized Spanish mackerel and, as he brought it up and over the railing, got an 'atta boy' from his neighbor a few yards away. These folks had no idea what had happened at the Blue Moon. They were just doing what they loved to do. Bait a hook, drop the line down into the Pass and look out over paradise. Pretty simple. Man, did I wish I were one of them. Oh to be standing there doing my thing in ignorant bliss. What the hell is going on, I thought. It didn't take long to find out.

I heard sirens in the distance. That told me Wayne was probably on the move. I wouldn't have thought the police would turn their sirens on to alert him if they knew he had parked his car. My guess was right. I heard the low-pitched roar of a speeding car approaching, and the piercing wail of the sirens was getting closer. I saw Wayne's car round the bend on the Boulevard just before the base of the bridge. He was flying. As the BMW ascended the bridge, I yelled in both directions, "Watch out for the car." It was tough to judge, but I figured he had to be doing at least sixty. As the car got closer, I noticed the passenger-side headlight and part of the fender were banged up. It was probably a slower speed casualty of eluding the pursuing sheriff's cruisers.

Wayne was straddling the double yellow line and hadn't slowed down at all as he crested the top of the bridge. An oncoming car heading north braked and swerved hard to the right to avoid a head-on collision. In doing so, the car skidded and jumped the curb, blowing out both right-side tires. Miraculously, no one on the bridge was hit, but it was a very close call for the guy directly opposite me who had just landed the fish. As he lurched away, he kicked over his bait bucket, tripped on his tackle box, and slid headlong on his chest and forearms. His hat and rod flew over the railing and down into the Pass.

Two trailing police cars started up the bridge but they clearly had reduced their speed. I turned and saw Wayne's BMW accelerating down the other side. When his car got to the bottom where the road was under construction, he lost control and the car skidded to the left, grazing one of the temporary concrete barriers. Wayne must have overcompensated from the impact, because he then veered sharply to the right and shot over into a storage lot for road construction equipment. Even over the blare of the sirens from the passing police cars, I heard a horrific crash that sent chills up and down my spine.

I took off down the bridge as fast as I could. On the way, my hat flew off my head but the leather straps caught my throat and saved me from losing it into the water below. As I raced off the bridge and turned into the sandy lot, I saw the two cruisers with lights still flashing stopped just behind Wayne's demolished BMW. He had skidded sideways through the storage area and smashed into a stack of concrete barriers. The policemen were looking into the car and I saw one of them shake his head to the other as I ran up. I was completely out of breath and was hyperventilating as I practically bullied my way between the officers. One of them grabbed me by the arm and said, "It's no use pal, he's dead."

The passenger-side impact had thrown Wayne, apparently with no seatbelt, across the front seats and partially out of the open window. His head and neck had crushed violently into the stacked barriers. He must have died instantly. What I could see of his contorted body was shocking and nauseating. Gasping hard for air from my sprint, and then seeing his crumpled form was too much. I staggered away a few paces and dry heaved four or five times.

After I got myself together, I walked slowly back up the bridge. The man who had nearly been hit had some scrapes and scratches, but he looked to be okay. The woman who had been driving the car that ended up on the sidewalk was pretty upset, but several of the others who had been fishing were trying to calm her down. The sound of more sirens could be heard in the distance. As I walked back down the other side of the bridge to my bike, yet another police car was approaching, followed by an ambulance and a fire engine. The public servants were really getting a workout on St. George Beach this evening, I thought.

I unlocked my bike and started heading home. I felt like a zombie. It seemed like all my senses had short-circuited and I was left in a numb fog. I was just going through the motions of riding my bike. As I turned onto my street and approached the house, I saw that the concrete manatee that held my mailbox had been demolished. Courtesy of Wayne's BMW, I figured. Still shook up from the events of the evening, I was unfazed by the damage. The sight of my garage helped to snap me out of my hypnotic trance. I realized it was Thursday evening and I had to call the supplier with my order for the standard Friday morning delivery.

# 18

When I woke up the next morning, I felt awful. Numerous gin and tonics had served as my dinner the night before. Heavy on the gin and light on the tonic. I had overdone it. I didn't normally drink much hard liquor, but I had rationalized it was the only thing that was going to provide me with any sleep, considering what I had witnessed. I had tossed them back until I passed out. The bigger mistake was not eating anything. Oh baby, did I have a whale of a headache. For breakfast, I forced down a couple pieces of toast and then washed down three aspirin with a big glass of spring water. Luckily, I survived a passing bout of nausea. There's nothing much worse than throwing up on the morning of a hangover. If you're going to have to go through that humbling experience, it's best to get it over with the night before and then get some sleep. I guess that way it gives your body a chance to recover.

It was a fortunate coincidence it was Friday, since that's the day I normally take off from exercising. Regardless of what day of the week it was, I wouldn't have been taking part in any form of physical activity. After my supplier showed up and delivered the order, I started to come around a little bit. A very little bit. Wow, I thought, two hangovers in one week. That hadn't happened in a long, long time. I thought back, and the last time might have been....I couldn't remember. Having even one in a week didn't happen very often at all. I couldn't be making a habit of that foolishness. I had to keep my mind centered on business at the cart, you know.

Since I hadn't spoken with Marie because she was working late at the Fountainhead the night before, I called her at home and filled her in on what had happened. She couldn't believe it. Number one, she couldn't believe Harry had been telling the truth about the whole thing. Number two, she couldn't believe Lisa had risked her marriage by cheating on Wayne. And number three, she couldn't believe the turn of events that had ended both of their lives. Marie thought of them as a couple who had everything and she couldn't comprehend it was over and that it was over so suddenly and completely. I told her I'd call her again when I had any information about funeral arrangements.

With great effort, I got the cart ready and made my way up the Boulevard to my spot at the beach access. The weather was picture perfect, with clear skies and low humidity, but my impairment restricted me from enjoying the conditions very much. Still, it was better to be up and moving around. If it had been a rainy day and I was stuck at home, it would have been easy to wallow around and end up feeling bad for a longer period of time. I had the morning newspaper with me, but I hadn't had the nerve to take it out of the plastic wrapper my paperboy rolled it up in each day.

A little after ten, the group of retirees came off the beach from their walk and, with their usual shenanigans, they perked up my mood a little. Their joking and kidding around helped distract me for a while from thinking about the fate of Lisa and Wayne McMillan. Here was a group of seniors who had lived full lives and yet were still full of life. They had been young once. They, no doubt, had faced some or all of the trials and tribulations of school, employment, relationships, and child rearing, and they had survived. They had made it to their golden years and they were making the most of it. What had done the trick for them? Was it purely mere perseverance in the face of different adversities throughout their lives, or was it some inner spirit that had kept them going? Having their health certainly was a big part of what made them tick. Maybe they had just been lucky or maybe they had made their own luck. I didn't know. What I did know was I envied them.

After the group left, I picked up the bag that held the newspaper. The daily paper was published up in the City of St. George, and many Beach residents complained that the island usually received very limited coverage. I unrolled the paper and saw, for this day at least, news from the Beach ruled the front page. The bold headline read: "Wife Murderer Dies in Crash." Below it were two large photographs. One was a picture of Wayne's mangled BMW. The other was the scene in front of the Blue Moon with all of the police cars and ambulances. In the doorway of the bar, talking to one of the sheriffs, damn if it wasn't Harry Forte, big as life. He'll be loving that, I thought. The accompanying article reported what had happened. As I read through it, Harry, the expert he envisioned himself to be, was quoted a couple of times as a witness. I concluded he wouldn't waste any time picking up a truckload of the day's edition of the St. George Press. What a ham.

Frank Olivetti came by on his way to the beach. He was pushing his crazy-looking cart, adorned with the stuffed money and pet parrot. "Yo, what's up, Ellis?" he said. "What the hell was all that about yesterday?"

"I take it you've seen the paper."

"Sure did," said Frank. "The St. George Press is having a field day with this story. The Beach is finally getting news coverage, but it's the wrong kind. Hey, you knew that guy, didn't you?"

"Yeah, I knew Wayne McMillan and his wife. I had the unfortunate experience of being at the Blue Moon when he shot her."

"No shit," said Frank. "I did see where your buddy, Harry Forte, was there from the article in the paper, but I didn't know you were."

"Yup, and it wasn't pretty. Then to top it off, I happened to be on the bridge down at Gateway Pass when Wayne wrecked his car and was killed.

"Man, you've been through it," he said. "Are you doing okay?"

"Well, between those two big messes and the five hundred gin and tonics I had last night, I'm feeling a little bit under the weather."

"That's too bad," said Frank. "Well, today's a new day. You'll come around."

"I'm banking on it."

"By the way," he said, "your boy, Harry, sure got a lot of ink in the paper. He was quoted all over the place."

"Yeah, he's a regular authority on this one. He'll be eating up the attention, trust me. I would have preferred to have not been around for any of it."

"I know what you mean," said Frank. "Look, Ellis, you hang in there."

"Thanks."

By the middle of the afternoon, my hangover symptoms faded and I started to feel almost like a human being again. Just before I started to close up, the loud blast of an air horn startled me. It was Harry, of course, driving the flatbed. He had stopped in the middle of the Boulevard, as he liked to do. "Yo, El," he called, "meet me at the Blue Moon in an hour. No excuses." He didn't even wait for an answer. Off he rumbled up the street.

I certainly wasn't in a drinking mood, but I figured it wouldn't be such a bad idea to return to the scene of the crime. At least I could find out about the latest info that was available. I dropped the cart at my house and drove up to the bar. As I walked in, I noticed some makeshift repairs had been done in the foyer area. There was a new piece of carpet and a fresh coat of paint on the wall. Nice touch, I thought. Good idea not to scare off the clientele with a blood-stained entryway. Tom was on duty behind the bar and he hailed me as I took a stool, "Well, hello there, stranger. Long time, no see."

"Yeah," I said, "I was in the area and thought I'd stop by and renew some old acquaintances. What's new?"

"Same do-do, different day," said Tom. "Draft, sir?"

"I'll try sipping on one," I said. "I kind of hurt myself last night, if you know what I mean."

"I do, indeed," he said drawing my beer from the palm tree tap. "I required a bit of a sleep aid last night as well."

I sensed someone behind me and turned to see Harry just in time to brace myself for his standard wallop on the back. "What's happening?" he boomed. For a change, we actually shook hands, and it turned into a firm, short-lived hug. That was good, because Harry was big and strong enough to break my ribs if he kept going.

"Oh, just another day in Oz," I replied. "How about you?"

"Same here," said Harry. "There's never any excitement around this place. Hey, Tommy, how about a draft. Oh, and nice job there at the entry. Like it never happened."

"Yes," said Tom, "Lydia saw to it that the area was spruced up a bit today."

Harry turned to me and said, "Where the hell did you get off to yesterday? You disappeared into thin air."

"Oh, you probably didn't notice me leave," I said. "You were pretty tied up with the authorities."

Tom set a beer in front of Harry and said, "Yes, Ellis, I believe we have a local celebrity in our midst. Dr. Harry was conversing with a number of dignitaries after the incident yesterday. You know, law enforcement officers, media, and the like."

"I've gathered that," I said. "I, however, had the poor timing of being on the bridge down at Gateway Pass when things went from bad to worse."

I proceeded to describe what went on, but I left out the part about seeing Wayne's car parked in my driveway. I didn't feel like being the recipient of any guilt trips on that decision. Based on the circumstances, I'd probably do same thing if it happened all over again. Harry had been Wayne's friend his whole life. I hadn't. If Harry had been there instead of me, I'm sure he would have tried to intervene. He had known Wayne long enough and well enough to take a chance on approaching him. Plus, Harry has a good bit of the ol' hero complex in him. He would have loved to take credit for being the one who resolved the crisis. I still didn't feel confident I could have made a difference. Considering Wayne's state of mind, any attempt to calm the violent maelstrom swirling inside him at the time was something that was out of my league.

"Well, what about the BMW?" asked Harry. "That car had every option in the book. Didn't the air bags go off? They could have saved him."

"You couldn't tell very well from the picture in the paper," I said, "but the car smacked sideways into the stack of concrete barriers. The airbags didn't inflate. I think Wayne had told me one time the sensors for those things are in the front of the car. He didn't have his seatbelt on anyway. Even if the airbags had gone off, he still could have been thrown around all over the place. The car was going fast as hell."

"Oh, man," said Harry. He sat there with a blank look on his face for a minute and then said, "I talked to my old man today. He said Wayne's service is at two o'clock tomorrow at Morgan's Funeral Home up in St. George. Visitation starts at one."

"Wow, that's fast," I said.

"Yeah," said Harry, "I think Wayne's mom wants to get this whole thing over with as soon as possible. My father said she's a wreck. I'm going to go see her in a little while. I've known her for a real long time. It's a damn good thing Wayne's father isn't still alive. This mess would break him in two. While he was still alive, he was really proud of what a big success Wayne had made of himself."

"What about Lisa?" I asked.

"Her parents are coming down from Michigan over the weekend to take care of the details," said Harry. "They're going to have her body sent back up there to be buried."

"I can't believe all of this," I said. Then after a pause, I nodded toward the front door of the Blue Moon, "Just about twenty-four hours ago, they were right over there and they both were alive."

"Yeah, it sucks," said Harry. "Hey, Tommy, let us have one more."

"Coming up," said Tom.

"One more is my limit today," I said.

Harry and I nursed our beers in silence. For the next ten or fifteen minutes, Tom, Harry and I glanced at each other several times, but instead of speaking, we each just shook our heads or looked away. It was the first time I could ever remember the three of us not have anything to say.

When I got up Saturday morning, I thought, what a difference a day makes when it comes to a hangover. I was well rested from a good night's sleep even though I'd had some strange dreams. No death or destruction, just some wacko scenes with a bunch of animated cartoon characters. That was a first. Very weird. I had called Marie at the Fountainhead before I went to bed and told her about the funeral for Wayne. Because the service was at two o'clock up in St. George, and we wanted to be there ahead of time, we both decided to take the whole day off.

I went over to the Gulf and got in a good swim. The combination of feeling better physically and yet still bearing a burning irritation from the tragedy made me really push it. I felt like I could have even given the dolphins a run for their money. I swam my ass off. When I got done, I felt exhilarated. There was nothing like a good workout to help vent some of the bad humors that were pent up inside me.

When I got back to the house I gave the Rosenbergs a call. Mildred answered and I proceeded to explain the events of Thursday evening. She and Irv had read the accounts in the newspaper from the day before, but they didn't know that Wayne McMillan and I had been friends. She told me they both were shaken by the story. It sure wasn't something that happened every day on St. George Beach. I made arrangements to see them after work on Sunday.

At twelve-thirty I picked up Marie. It was very unusual for us to be so dressed up. In general, the fashion in Florida is pretty casual. I was wearing the only suit I owned. It was reserved for weddings and funerals, neither of which I attended very often. Marie had on a dark print dress and heels. She looked beautiful. If I hadn't known better, I could have fallen for her right there on the spot.

The drive up to St. George went smoothly with the lighter weekend traffic. It was a perfect day, weatherwise, sunny and warm with a light breeze. Living where the weather is nice most of the time, it's easy to occasionally take a beautiful day for granted. Probably due to the fact we were going to a funeral, today was one of those days. During the ride, Marie and I were fairly quiet. I don't think either of us wanted to come face to face with the realization of what we were doing. If we didn't talk about it, maybe it wasn't actually happening.

The old road up into St. George is very scenic. It is primarily a residential stretch with well-maintained homes of an earlier vintage. Mature royal palms line both sides of the street for miles. Of all the types of palm trees, I particularly like the royal variety. Their trunks stand very straight and are a gray concrete color. They almost look as if they are poured masonry telephone poles with green fronds adorning the top. Even considering the length of time I had lived in the area, I was still impressed with their statuesque appearance. In an odd way, it was like we were driving between two of the world's largest picket fences. My paradise helped to keep my imagination alive.

We found the funeral home without any trouble. It was a Spanish-style building with white stucco walls and a terra cotta tile roof. Between the windows were flat tile patterns in blue, green and aquamarine colors. The property was spacious and attractively landscaped. As funeral homes go, the place was nice. When we pulled in, I saw Harry and his wife Brenda standing outside the entrance talking with Tom. Marie knew the guys and had met Brenda a couple of times. Brenda is tall and dark-haired, with a sturdy figure. She is a no-nonsense kind of person, straightforward with no hidden agendas. What you saw was what you got with her. For crying out loud, she had to put up with Harry. That was a major project in itself.

As Marie and I walked up, I said, "Greetings, folks. Is it me, or does it seem a little unusual for the five of us to be standing here in our Sunday-go-to-meeting clothes?"

"Unusual, indeed," said Tom, "on this fine Saturday afternoon. Although, I dare say we make a handsome group decked out in our full regalia."

"Well, this sure isn't my idea of fun," groused Harry. "Oh, the reception after the funeral is at my parents' house. They've got a lot more room than Mrs. McMillan does. My old man wanted to do something to help her out. He's having it catered. The works."

"That's nice," I said.

"My father just lost the top realtor he had," said Harry. "Wayne kicked butt." Harry went on to tell us Wayne was buried privately earlier in the day and only family members had attended. It had been Mrs. McMillan's wish to keep things as low-key as possible.

We stood around and made small talk for a few minutes until Tom said, "I think it best if we made our way inside and offered our condolences to Mrs. McMillan. Although, I do expect it to be a melancholy experience. I happen to have additional tissues in my possession, should anyone require

140

them. Please don't be shy to request them if the need arises."

As we were about to walk in, I pointed out that Roger Carson was pulling into the parking lot. Tommy said he told Roger about the service the night before at the Blue Moon. We waited for Roger and the six of us walked in together. In the receiving line with Mrs. McMillan were Wayne's brother and two sisters, along with their spouses. I had never met any of them, which made things a little confusing. I had to ask Harry for help in identifying who was who. We each, in turn, greeted Mrs. McMillan and said how sorry we were, but I doubted she would remember much of the whole ordeal. It was clear she had taken some medication intended to ease the pain she had to be feeling. All things considered, it was probably the best thing for her to do.

After we went through the line, our group sat together as the parlor filled up. Two rows of dark wooden pillars ran the length of the room. The pillars were intricately carved and supported large exposed beams that spanned the ceiling. Massive pots of ferns lined the side walls between the windows. It would have been a peaceful and comfortable place had it not been for the reason we were there.

The gathering consisted of only about a hundred people. The hastiness of the arrangements and the circumstances of Wayne's death helped to keep the attendance to a modest number. As I looked around the assemblage of Wayne's friends, relatives, and work associates, it occurred to me that the six of us didn't quite fit into the refined mold of the other mourners. Well, at least the guys. Marie and Brenda could have blended in with any group.

Since Wayne hadn't been a churchgoer, to offer the service, Mrs. McMillan had enlisted the minister from the church she attended. He was an elderly man who we found had a flair for the dramatic. Throughout the service, he spoke a sentence or two and then took a long pause for emphasis. He began by saying he really hadn't known Wayne. I hated that. I don't know how many funerals I've been to where the person running the show didn't even know the deceased. Too many for me, anyway. It would have been far better if Harry's father or a relative had delivered the eulogy. At least someone who knew Wayne could have related some firsthand accounts about his life. Shoot, Harry himself would have been an improvement, even if some of the stories he told weren't completely true.

The minister went on to say what a tragedy it was to lose Wayne at such a young age. He tried to justify everything by saying God works in strange ways and there was a reason for everything. I guess he was trying to comfort us all, but I didn't feel very comforted. I would have rather seen someone who knew Wayne stand up there and say, "Wayne's gone and I don't like it." I kind of had a feeling it was the way most of the other people felt, too. It was sad and it was frustrating.

We hung in there and did some of the standard funeral things. We sang a couple of hymns and the minister read some passages from the Bible. Heck, the minister could have read the whole darn

Bible to us and I don't think it would have made anyone feel much better. Thinking about Wayne and what he was really like made the whole religious atmosphere seem inappropriate, but we got through it. It was just awful that Wayne was gone and there wasn't anything, short of a few funny stories about his life, which would have helped to change the dreadful mood everyone was in. With the congregation reflecting on the shocking loss of Wayne, by the end of the service there wasn't a dry eye in the house. Harry included. Me included. Tommy kept busy passing out tissues. When it was finally over, Mr. Forte announced that everyone was invited to his house for refreshments.

In almost formal procession, we drove to the Forte residence, which was nearby. The place could best be described as palatial. Considering it was located within the city limits of St. George, the property was extensive. The spacious acreage had numerous palm trees and shrubs, and the overall landscaping was meticulously manicured. The large two-story house had pale pink stucco walls and a slate shingled roof. Four tall white columns on the front porch bolstered the second floor overhang, and all of the windows were framed with ornate cypress trim. There also was a separate four-car garage. To the rear of the property ran the Sovereign River, which at its western end emptied into the Gulf of Mexico. Harry told me on an earlier occasion that his parents had lived in the house for about eight years. The real estate business had made Mr. Forte a wealthy man. But he didn't just hand the dough out to his kids. It wasn't that he hoarded it, but he maintained the conservative ethic that you worked for your money.

Harry's two older sisters were married and neither of them had ever been involved in the family business. Harry's younger brother did work in an administrative capacity at the real estate agency's main office. Harry had previously indicated, however, that his brother did not possess the business savvy or drive of their father. I felt sure it was safe to say that all of the siblings were welcome in their parents' house at any time to share in the fruits of success. But the bottom line was Mr. Forte kept a close rein on his finances like any wise businessman. He was prepared for a rainy day. In reality, none of the kids were making a living by mooching off the old man.

We were directed to park our cars on an angle off the side of the long driveway. The sight of my beat-up van, as well as Harry and Tom's pickup trucks, parked amongst expensive Mercedes', Cadillacs, and other luxury cars, seemed like a humorous contradiction. Perhaps the funniest vehicle was Roger Carson's old Ford station wagon, complete with imitation wood-grained side panels. The car was huge. It wasn't in very good shape and easily visible inside were fishing supplies for his boat filling every available square inch. Roger had pulled the wagon a little too far off of the driveway and the front bumper was nestled in a fern-like bush. I needled him as we got out, "What's your car doing in the shrubbery, Roger?"

"Feeding," he said in a calm voice and with a straight face. As serious as he normally was, at times, Roger could be a real kidder.

We followed a flagstone path around to the rear of the house. On the patio beside the huge kidney-shaped swimming pool, the caterer had erected a large white tent. Beneath it was the most sumptuous buffet of appetizers I had ever seen. Serving as the centerpiece was an immense mound of cleaned jumbo shrimp atop a bed of shaved ice. Surrounding that shrine to the seafood world was every fresh salad item imaginable. I believe that's referred to as crudités. But what do I know? I'm just a beach vendor. Waitresses circulated, carrying trays of caviar and other exotic hors d'oeuvres. I had no idea what some of the stuff was. There was even a guy shucking fresh oysters. The bar, which was set up at the end of the tent, was crowded with bottles of nothing but top-shelf liquors. I leaned over to Marie and said, "Pretty nice spread, huh?"

"Yeah," she said, quietly. "Very nice."

"What would you like to drink?"

"Well," said Marie, "ordinarily I would probably just have a glass of wine, but considering the setup on that bar, I think I'll have a gin and tonic. Don't bother specifying a brand. I'm sure they're all really good."

"I'd have one of those, too," I said, "but I really maxed out on them Thursday night. I think I'm going to stay with beer today."

Our gang stuck together as we sipped on our drinks. Each of us filled a small plate with a variety of appetizers. Each of us except Harry, that is. Holding his rum and coke in one hand, he proceeded to graze around the buffet table, sampling one delicacy after another without bothering to get a plate. Brenda saw what he was doing and was about to correct him, but Harry's mother beat her to it. Mrs. Forte confronted Harry and quietly but firmly chided him about his manners. The two of them turned away from the table together, and it provided Harry the opportunity to introduce his mother to the rest of us.

Mrs. Forte looked to be in her late fifties and everything about her appearance was proper and precise. I wouldn't say she was petite, but her less-than-average size made you wonder how she could possibly be Harry's mother, as big as he was. She had a warm smile and was gracious and friendly. The wealth that had come to her marriage had not made her one bit conceited or condescending. One by one, Mrs. Forte engaged us in conversation. She showed genuine interest in meeting each of us and she was eager to learn our various occupations. She was curious and attentive and it was clear she wasn't just putting on the social graces without meaning it. Mrs. Forte was a very nice lady.

As more people made their way to the buffet area, our band of six drifted over near the pool. We were all so nicely dressed I couldn't help but compliment everyone's attire. After I made admiring comments to the girls, I said to Harry, "That's a sharp-looking suit and tie you're wearing there, big guy."

"Thanks," said Harry, "I bought this when Brenda and I were in Hawaii last fall. They have some first-class clothes there from all over the world. They're not cheap, but they're primo quality."

"Hey, Harry," I said, "there was something missing from the service today and it bothered me. No one stood up and told any humorous stories about Wayne. It would have helped break up the somber atmosphere. Tell us a good story about Wayne when you guys were younger."

Harry thought for a minute and then said, "Okay, here's one. Right after we both turned twenty-one, we were down at the Beach one night hitting different bars and checking out the babes. We finally ended up in this pizza joint 'cause we were starving. We worked on a pitcher while we waited for the pizza and I could tell that Wayne was starting to lose it. I was glad I was driving. Well, the pizza finally shows up and, for Wayne, it was too little too late. He's sitting there chewing on the pizza with his eyes closed. Then he reaches down for his mug of beer and grabs the oregano shaker by mistake. He hoists it up to take a drink, thinking it's his beer, and a bunch of oregano comes flying out on his face. Even when we walked out of the place, he still had oregano all over his face. It was too funny to say anything to him. We get outside and I tell him to stay put while I go down the street to get my truck. I figured it wouldn't look very good for the cops to see him staggering all over the place. So I get my truck and go around the block and come into the parking lot right behind him. He's standing on the sidewalk, leaning half over, looking down the street for me, and I'm parked like three feet behind him. He had no clue I was there. I just sat there for a few minutes laughing my ass off. Finally, I tooted the horn and he jumped a mile in the air. Then he got in and I took him home. Every now and then ever since that night, one of us would bring up that story and we'd have a big hoot about it."

As we all laughed, I said, "Harry, a story like that at the service is more like what I had in mind. Although I'd bet Mrs. McMillan might not have cared too much for one with all the drinking. But I do think everybody could have used a good laugh to cut through the emotions we were feeling. It would have made the whole thing a lot more palatable."

As we continued to talk about Wayne, Mr. Forte walked up and Harry introduced us all. Harry's dad was tall and distinguished-looking with graying hair, but he didn't have nearly the thick build of his elder son. I guess Harry enjoyed food to a far greater extent than either of his parents. Mr. Forte was polite enough, but he didn't talk to each of us individually the way Mrs. Forte had. Because he knew we were all friends of Harry's, I think it might have made him a little more tentative. He probably viewed us as dangerous territory for potentially rowdy behavior. We were all dressed up and were showing good manners, but, in his eyes, we were probably all guilty in advance by our association with Harry.

As Mr. Forte left the circle, Marie took the opportunity to excuse herself, and Brenda followed suit. I heard Brenda say to Marie, "Come on in with me and I'll show you the house." I felt certain that was exactly what Marie was hoping for as they went inside.

Harry then announced, "I'll be right back. I've got to hit the head."

Roger called after him, "What do you mean 'head?' Do you think you're out on a boat or something?"

"Yeah, man," said Harry as he walked away.

Tom, Roger, and I walked over to the bar for a refill. As we passed the buffet table I asked Tom about the term crudités for the fresh vegetables. If anybody in our group would know the answer, I knew it would be him. I pronounced it *cru-dite*. He said, "Well, you're close. The word actually has three syllables, not two. It's spelled c-r-u-d-i-t-é-s with the accent over the 'e', and is pronounced *kroo-di-tae*. The 's' is silent. The word is of French origin and has only made it into English language dictionaries in recent years. It is defined as cut raw vegetables served as an appetizer."

Roger, who had been listening, blurted out, "You're amazing, Tommy, you know that?"

"Thank you, sir," said Tom, "I strive to be as thorough as possible. And I might add that the overall array of food and drink here today would be an Epicurean's dream."

Roger leaned over to me and mumbled, "I'm not going to touch that one with a ten-foot pole."

Tommy and I were drinking beer but I noticed Roger had been drinking a brown-colored cocktail. When he asked the bartender for a Jack Daniels on the rocks, I was floored. I nudged Roger in the side and said, "Since when do you drink anything but beer, and then nurse that to boot?"

"I figured," said Roger, "I'd have something a little stronger today in honor of our departed friend. I didn't know him as well as you guys, but I still miss him anyway."

We chatted and nibbled some more, and after a bit Brenda came back out of the house. With a knowing smile, she said, "Well, Ellis, Marie was really impressed with the house, but I think she's even more impressed with the guy she's talking to in there. Harry just told me his name is Andrew Martin."

"Oh, is that right?" I said.

"Yup," said Brenda. "Harry said he was a friend of Wayne's from the Country Club. They used to play tennis together. The guy's a dentist and he was divorced about a year ago."

"Oh, really?" I said. "An available man with money is right up Marie's alley."

"Well," said Brenda, nodding toward the back of the house, "they really seem to be hitting it off."

I turned and, through the French doors that lined the length of the patio, saw Marie conversing with a tall, dark-haired, well-dressed guy who was probably in his thirties. She tossed her head back laughing, then touched his arm and continued talking with a smile. It wasn't difficult to see there was an immediate attraction between them.

"I could be wrong," I said, "but Dr. Martin could be Marie's ticket to success if she plays her cards right."

"You bet," said Brenda. "Just what the doctor ordered."

We both laughed and then I excused myself to use the facilities. I stepped into the house, and as I passed behind Marie's new acquaintance, she caught a glimpse of me. I gave her a smile and a wink without stopping to speak. On my return trip from the bathroom I chose a different route so I wouldn't disrupt her conversation.

I went out onto the patio and talked with Brenda, Tom, and Roger for a while. Harry was circulating around, speaking to some old friends he and Wayne had known from high school. Around six o'clock, Tom suggested we should consider leaving. I caught Marie's eye through the glass doors and she came out of the house.

"We're getting ready to leave," I said. "I thought I might have to come in and drag you out of there. So how are things going with Mr. Right?"

"Well," she said, "actually they're going very well. He just asked me to go out to dinner from here and I said yes."

"Well, how about that," I said. "This is the first time I ever got dumped at a funeral."

"Look, he's really a nice guy," said Marie.

"I bet he seemed even nicer when you found out he's a dentist."

"Ellis," she said, "I'm not going let this chance slip away. I just want to go out with him and see what happens. I think he likes me."

"What's not to like, Marie," I said. "You've got a head on your shoulders and you look great. Go for it."

"Thanks, Ellis," she said, "I'll let you know how things turn out."

She turned and, with a spring in her step, went back inside. The rest of us decided to retire to the Blue Moon for further refreshments. Harry told Tom, Roger, and me to go on ahead. He and Brenda would be along in a little while.

Tommy led our caravan out of the driveway in his pickup and Roger followed in his station wagon. I brought up the rear in my van. I wanted to keep Roger in the middle so we didn't lose him. I'd seen him have much more to drink than I ever had, and I wanted to keep an eye on him.

# 21

I was glad it was still light out for the drive to the Blue Moon. Tommy held a steady course and maintained a constant speed. Roger, however, tended to frequently slow down and then accelerate to catch up to Tommy's pickup. He also drifted to the right more than a few times. By being in the middle of our little convoy, Roger was somewhat protected from being observed by any officers of the highway patrol. In trucker lingo, it meant he was in the rocking chair. There was already a seed planted in my mind that told me Roger shouldn't drive any further than the bar.

When we rolled into the parking lot of the Blue Moon, Roger was slow to get out of his car. I approached Tom and said, "I think it's a good idea if this is as far as the Captain drives tonight. He was weaving quite a bit on the ride down here."

"Based on what I observed," said Tom, "I believe that is an accurate assessment. Let's keep it in mind as the evening progresses."

Roger finally emerged from his car and, as the three of us walked toward the entrance, I said, "Cap'n Roger, what do you say if we all get a sandwich in here. It might perk us up a little."

"Sounds good to me," said Roger, slowly forming his words. "Those appetizers were tasty but they don't fill you up."

Lydia was behind the bar as we walked in. She was making a rare Saturday appearance by filling in for Tom. Her face brightened when she saw us taking our seats at the bar.

"My, my," she said, "let me look at the three of you, all gussied up. A single gal would have a tough time choosing between you sharp-looking hunks."

"Oh, really?" I said. "I know a single gal that just managed to get away from us."

"What do you mean, Ellis?" said Lydia.

"Oh nothing, Lydia," I said. "I was just kidding around. I guess we'll have a pitcher when you get a chance."

"So how did things go up there in town today?" she asked, drawing beer from the palm tree tap.

"All in all it went okay," I said. "It had its ups and downs."

"The high point," said Tom, "was that we were privileged to attend a reception after the service at our dear Harry's parents' house. Or should I say, estate."

"Pretty swanky, eh?" asked Lydia. "The place lousy with money?"

"Swanky, indeed," said Tom. "Harry does a fine job of camouflaging his lineage."

I turned to Tom and said, "You know, you probably could say something like that about us too, huh, Tommy."

"You may have a valid point there, my friend," said Tom.

"Say, Lydia," I said, "how about three of your fish sandwiches. We're in need of a little fortification."

"No problem at all, fellas," she said. "You know we've got the freshest grouper on the island."

Tom straightened on his stool and said, "You know, Lydia, I'm starting to like the view from this side of the bar. They do say that work is the curse of the drinking class."

"Is that so?" she replied. "Well, just don't get too comfortable over there. You'll be back on this side tomorrow. I don't want you to do too much relaxing."

"Well," said Tom, "I believe it was Hemingway who wrote that in the southern climates people drink for pleasure, and in the northern climates they drink to avoid depression. At last check, I believe we are in the southern part of Florida, so I intend to enjoy myself for as long as possible. I may just decide to become a regular patron of this fine establishment instead of enduring the arduous hardships of being on that side of the bar."

Lydia just shook her head and walked back into the kitchen. Because of the length of time Tommy had worked at the Blue Moon, Lydia knew him inside and out. She took his little wisecracks without letting it get under her skin. She knew him better than anyone and realized he was a dedicated employee she could depend on without fail.

The sun, which was visible through the windows at the back of the bar, was beginning to sink low over the Gulf. Hanging fronds from the palm trees on the beach swayed gently and were silhouetted against the ever-enlarging ball of orange light. The approaching sunset, although occurring at varying times throughout the year, seems to produce a calming effect on those who take the time to enjoy it. It is mesmerizing in much the same way as watching wood burn in a fireplace or campfire. The three of us took in the natural beauty without speaking. Our serenity was cut short when Harry, entering the bar with Brenda, bellowed, "It's going to be a hell of a sunset."

Startled, I turned and said, "Thanks for the warning, Harry."

The loud interruption had done several things. First, I noticed it had jolted Roger awake from an unscheduled nap. Second, it had saved us from Harry's customary slap on the back, which none of us would have been prepared for. As Harry and Brenda took seats next to us at the bar, Lydia served our sandwiches. I leaned over to Roger and whispered, "While we're eating, how about if you give me your phone number. I'll call your wife and ask her to come give you a ride home."

Without any display of stubbornness, Roger obliged. I went outside to the pay phone and, as I picked up the receiver, I chuckled to myself that it was fortunate there wasn't a big dog tied to it. I called Roger's wife, Eleanor, and explained the situation. I had only met her several times over the years, and I knew she was very quiet and shy. Eleanor immediately grasped the necessity of her assistance and said she would be right over. As I hung up the phone, two large vans were pulling into the parking lot. It was the members of the band Attitude Blue. After coming to a stop, the back door of one of the vans swung open and Lil' Luther popped out. He was dressed in his same suit but, as usual, it looked cleaned and pressed. He recognized me and walked right over.

"Good evening, sir," he said. "You're sure dressed up tonight."

"Hi there, Luther," I said. "I had to go to this formal thing today. How are things with you?"

"Well, sir," said Luther, "I have good news."

"Oh yeah?" I said. "That's great. I could use some good news. What's up?"

Luther's face broke into a broad smile. He was beaming when he said, "My mother called my aunt down here in St.George and they've decided to drive with me up to Memphis next month. My mother was talking to a friend where she works who knows a family that lives there. She checked with them and they said it's okay for the three of us to stay at their house. The folks in Memphis have a nephew who plays drums in a blues band. It may seem like kind of a roundabout connection, but it's a chance to get my foot in the door up there. I'm pretty excited about it. I can't wait."

"Luther, that's great. I've always heard that May is the top month for blues in Memphis. They have a big festival with bands coming in from all over. I'm really happy for you. This could be the opportunity for you we talked about before."

"I want to thank you," said Luther, "for all the things you've said to me while I've been down here. It's helped my confidence. But I am sorry to tell you that tonight is my last night here at the Blue Moon. I'm going back up to Gainesville tomorrow."

"That's okay," I said. "I will miss hearing you play, but I think you're doing the right thing. Maybe I'll get to see you again sometime on television. Just promise me you won't hold anything back tonight. Let 'er rip."

"You got it, and thanks again," said Luther as we shook hands and I gave him a pat on the shoulder.

While Luther went over to help the band with their equipment, I walked down along the side of the building and stood by the bicycle rack. I watched the setting sun, now yet even larger on the horizon, slowly dip down and finally disappear beyond the waters of the Gulf. I heard the faint applause of a group of people on the beach who were showing their appreciation of Mother Nature's beauty. Although it wasn't my normal practice to do it, I quietly clapped my hands twice, then turned and walked back inside.

I went over to Roger and, in a hushed voice, told him his wife would be coming by soon to give him a ride home. He gave a nod of approval. As I sat down on my stool, I noticed my plate with the fish sandwich was missing. I looked over and saw Harry wipe his mouth with a napkin, crumple up the napkin, and then drop it on an empty plate in front of him. He cleared his throat and said, "You were gone for so long, and I didn't want your food to get cold. I did you a favor and ate it." Then he raised his hand and called, "Yo, Lydia, how about getting Ellis another fish sandwich."

"Sure thing, Harry," said Lydia. "Anything else?"

"Yeah, I'll take another rum and coke. How about making it a double this time. And a round on me for our gang here."

The band began filing in and setting up their equipment. While I was waiting for my replacement sandwich, I went over and kept an eye out the front window for Roger's wife. Roger told me she drove a blue two-door Dodge Aries. As I stood there, a wave of sadness came washing over me. I remembered it was exactly where I was standing with Harry only two days earlier when Wayne had put an end to Lisa's life. I was still having trouble dealing with the sorrowful aftermath of the whole affair and it started to get the best of me. I squinted my eyes together and, with a barely audible sigh, murmured, "Shit." As I continued to look through the window, I got a grip on my emotions. With puffed cheeks, I blew out a long breath of air.

In a few minutes, the car Roger had described pulled into the entrance of the Blue Moon. I went over and put my hand on Roger's shoulder and told him his wife had arrived. As he stood up, he placed a twenty-dollar bill on the bar and said goodbye to everyone. I was about to walk out with him when Lydia delivered my new sandwich. Tom got up and told me to stay and eat. He accompanied Roger, but without giving him any assistance. The food had helped Roger come around a little and he walked in a slow, steady pace to the door. I think, considering his age and the day's activities, he was plain worn out. Tom stayed with Roger on the way out to Eleanor's car more for moral, rather than physical, support.

## 22

After preparing their equipment and tuning their guitars, Lil' Luther and Attitude Blue started out the first set with an instrumental. Having now played together a number of times, they seemed to have jelled even more than the last time I had seen them. It was obvious Luther was still the class of the outfit, though. He continued to be the front man of the group by introducing the songs. Perhaps because this would be the last time they would play with Luther, the other members of the band all wore an intent look on their faces and they played with enthusiasm. This was as close to stardom as any of them would ever get. However, their short association with Luther seemed to help boost their performance level for the present and, most likely, beyond.

Most people normally associate the blues with black musicians. Granted, the roots of blues music are planted firmly in the cotton fields of the Mississippi Delta, and blues origins lie historically with black artists. But in more recent years, many white performers have proven their talent for playing the blues. Whether intentional or not, Lil' Luther began rambling through the first set with a succession of music by white guitarists. He went back to back to back with songs by Eric Clapton, George Thorogood, and Paul Butterfield.

When it came to precision this night, Luther did not disappoint. He played and sang with an almost overwhelming energy and he displayed an amazing stage presence. His efforts were not wasted on the ever-increasing crowd. Loud applause followed the end of every song. Word had clearly circulated since his earlier appearances at the Blue Moon, and it was reflected in the turnout. By nine o'clock the place was packed.

Tommy and I slid over closer to Brenda and Harry to make more space at the bar. All of the tables had been taken and a growing number of standees, looking for drinks, took turns elbowing their way between customers who filled every available barstool. I had never seen the Blue Moon nearly as crowded, and it tested Lydia's ability to keep up with the demand for drinks. She was toiling like a beaver but she didn't seem to mind a bit. If she could have Luther playing every night, her bar would become a gold mine in no time.

During the first set, Tom and I paced ourselves with a couple of beers. Brenda was not much of a drinker, and after a glass of wine early on, she sipped on a bottle of spring water. Harry, on the other hand, had not let up on a torrid run of rum and cokes. His physical size helped give him a greater capacity for alcohol, but I knew he had to be reaching even his extended limit. I think the experience of losing his lifelong friend had driven him to work hard at rinsing away the anguish he had to be feeling. Harry certainly displayed a tough, armorlike exterior, but those close to him knew he had a caring heart beating deep inside. He was the kind of guy who would do anything for a friend in need. It didn't take a genius to realize he was hurting from the loss of Wayne.

Luther ended the first set with a moving version of B.B. King's, "The Thrill Is Gone." My mind couldn't help but drift to thoughts of Wayne and Lisa as I listened. Even though they had been on the opposite end of the financial scale from the characters normally described in blues songs, there was a similarity to their situation in the central theme of the music. When the song ended and the band took a break, it gave the four of us the opportunity to talk.

"Luther really has them packed in here tonight," I said.

"And with good reason," said Tom. "Apparently the inhabitants of our fair region know good music when they hear it. If Lil' Luther keeps playing here, Lydia will retire a millionaire in under six months."

"Unfortunately," I said, "tonight's his last night. He told me outside earlier that he's leaving tomorrow to go back up to Gainesville. He's going up to Memphis next month to try to get in with a band up there."

"That," said Tom, "should not be a difficult undertaking for such a skilled musician."

Brenda leaned over and said, "I think the blues are great, especially the way Luther plays them. Even the slow songs make you want to tap your foot."

"What I find interesting with the blues," said Tom, "is the lyrics. Almost every line is repeated. I suppose that's in case you didn't get it the first time." Then leaning over me toward Harry, "That would make it so even you can understand it, my dear Harry."

"Real funny, Tommy," said Harry shaking his fist in the air. "Understand this."

"Just kidding, my good man," said Tom. "But, in some ways, I do see a similarity in the disheartened and dismal lyrics of blues songs, with that of country music. It seems in both genres, the singer is telling a grief-stricken tale of bereavement from losing his woman."

Harry leaned over and, with bloodshot eyes and slurred words, said, "Who says it's not the man's fault, anyway? Even if a guy's not rich or even very good-looking, if he treats his woman right, she probably wouldn't have left him in the first place."

There were blank stares and pauses for reflection among the rest of us that were finally broken by Tommy, saying, "That, Dr. Harry, is perhaps the most astute observation I believe I have ever heard you make."

"Thank you," said Harry, with a slight bow. "I'm not chopped liver over here. You know what I mean? Come to think of it, Tommy, didn't you have something like that happen with your girlfriend, way back when?"

"To be honest," said Tom, "I must say that is, in fact, true. However, I don't make a habit of discussing it. But having been thoroughly relaxed by today's drinking extravaganza, I must admit that I have experienced the blues, if you will, on a firsthand basis. Back in college at Clemson, I had the same girlfriend for all four years of undergraduate school and then for my one year in the Master's program. During grad school, she had begun to pressure me a bit for some form of commitment for the future that I wasn't ready or willing to provide. It may have been her way of testing me. I think she didn't see me as being mature enough or ambitious enough to meet her expectations, and at the time, she probably was right. In any event, she dropped me like a hot potato and started dating a guy I knew from another fraternity. I must say I immediately fell into a miserable and morose state of depression. In my mind, it was as if I was constantly watching a movie of the two of them together, doing the things that lovers do. It was a heartsick, anguished form of self-pity that I have never forgotten, and doubt I will ever completely put out of my mind. Some months later I saw her at a party. I had heard she was pregnant and that they were going to get married. The sight of her in the *family way* succinctly and decisively confirmed what I had been imagining all along. And that, my friends, is having the blues."

"Wow," said Brenda, "I'm sorry to hear that, Tom. I hope you've gotten over her."

"The years," said Tom, "have enabled my mental movie to dim to black-and-white. I have not, however, been able to have a sustained relationship with a woman ever since, it seems. It's probably just me. So, Harry, perhaps you are indeed correct. Treat your woman right and she won't leave you."

"That," said Harry, "will be fifty dollars for the office visit."

"Send me a bill," said Tom.

Tommy had mentioned bits and pieces of that story to me a few times, but it was a number of years earlier, probably soon after he started working at the Blue Moon. Nobody else had ever said anything to me about it, and I knew for sure I'd never heard such a detailed description of a dark part of Tom's past. I hadn't known that it weighed so heavily on him. It made me feel that I wasn't alone when it came to problems with women when I was younger. Unfortunately, the contrary results had stuck with both Tommy and me.

The four of us spent the balance of the musical break taking turns going to the restroom. We wanted to make sure we maintained the beachhead we had established at the crowded bar. On my trip to the men's room, a line of three or four guys was backed up inside the door. As I waited my turn, several more fellows came in behind me. Just as I completed my business, Harry came blasting through the door. Apparently not noticing the others waiting, Harry proceeded to cut in front of the group and use the fixture I had just vacated. His size and boldness must have intimidated the others because not one of those in line said a word. I laughed to myself as I went back to the bar. Harry was on a roll.

Luther and Attitude Blue opened the second set with an easy-flowing version of a song previously done by Little Junior Parker, "Next Time You See Me." The upbeat nature of the music belied the harshness of the lyrics. The singer warns his woman that changes in their relationship are coming and the fault of any negative effects lies with her with the repeated line, "And if it hurts you my darlin', you only have yourself to blame." The song went on to say that the woman has been untruthful and unfaithful and she is responsible for anything bad that may happen. Luther played it to the hilt. The crowd really liked that one. Hoots, hollers, and whistles could be heard over the applause.

Lil' Luther continued to show his versatility. On some other songs he had come across with a gravelly, earthy voice, but on that number he employed a smooth and fluid style. He could do it all. Luther continued the set with songs done by John Lee Hooker, Howlin' Wolf, Bo Diddley and Albert King, to name a few. It seemed like there was no limit to what Luther could do and do well. The guys in Attitude Blue were on their best game also. They were playing their butts off.

To mix in a song that espoused the good virtues of love rather than the down side, Luther ended the second set with the song "Grits Ain't Groceries," which declares: "If I don't love you baby, grits ain't grocery, eggs ain't poultry, and Mona Lisa was a man." I'd say that is making a statement. With the tune's freewheeling rhythm and bold statements of devotion, Luther had managed to incite the crowd into a happily frenzied mob. It was safe to say that St. George Beach and even all of the City of St. George itself had never seen a blues show quite like what we were being treated to. It was draining.

During the second break, we got a chance to catch our breath. With the combination of the funeral service, the reception afterward, and the evening's entertainment, we all were starting to run out of gas. It looked like Harry was starting to nod out on his barstool. Brenda was by far the most alert of all of us. She turned to Tom and me saying, "I don't know what it is about the blues, whether it's the rhythm or all those high notes, but it puts you in a sexy mood."

"I know what you mean," I said. "The blues are pretty basic. Most of the songs are about either wanting or not wanting the opposite sex. I guess that's what life is all about. The rest is just details."

"Indeed," said Tom, "the blues tend to have a carnal quality to them. They seem to stress the absence of intellectual and moral influence. In turn, they have a preoccupation with gratifying the bodily senses."

I was waiting for Harry to make a crack like, "gratify this," but I looked over and noticed he had fallen asleep. He didn't have his head on the bar and, in fact, he didn't even have his hands on the bar. He was sitting upright with his arms at his sides and his chin resting on his chest. It was the oddest position to be out cold, but he looked as steady as the Rock of Gibraltar. Tommy took the opportunity to get a dig in, saying, "It looks like our dear Harry is displaying the attributes of a vampire bat at rest over there. Albeit a very large bat."

After glancing at Harry, Brenda shook her head and went on, "The words are a lot about falling out of love and yet wanting love. I guess that's when you're feeling the most alive."

"Maybe," I said, "you have to have had the blues really bad sometime to get a feeling for the whole thing."

"That could be true," said Brenda, "but I think it's the combination of the words and the music that makes you feel sexy."

"I dare say," said Tom, "by the looks of your man Harry there, you better file any sensual feelings you may have until tomorrow, or find an alternative partner this evening."

The three of us had a good laugh and, almost on cue, Harry's eyes opened and he was awake. Brenda patted him on the back and said, "Come on, big boy, it's time for me to take you home."

"No problem," slurred Harry, "I can drive."

"I don't think so," said Brenda.

"What do you mean?" said Harry. "I got you here, I'll get you home."

"Harry," I said, "I'd advise you to use that thick head of yours and let Brenda do the driving. You've had a busy day. We all have. I think it's time all of us went home and got some sleep."

Tommy got Lydia's attention and we settled up. Even though Lydia had her hands full with the large crowd, she made a point to briefly thank us for coming in. She was well aware that there was a clear difference between the newcomers who were at the Blue Moon just to listen to Luther, and her steady, repeat customers. When Luther was gone, so would be most of the throng of patrons. Lydia knew who the regulars were, and she appreciated them. She took the time to show it.

We went out to the parking lot and, without any resistance, loaded Harry in the passenger seat of his truck. Brenda got behind the wheel and, as she started the engine, I said, "Looks like you're toting a heavy load there, Brenda."

Harry leaned over on her and said out the window, "Like Jack Nicholson said in the movie Goin' South, 'I have my faults, I admit it, but I got my ways, too.'"

"That you do, big fella," said Tommy, and then to Brenda, "Is everything okay?"

"I'll manage," said Brenda. "I've got a lot of experience."

"I bet you have," said Tommy, and then whispering closely to Brenda, "It might be a good idea to try and calm down Harry's intake just a bit though. If he keeps it up like this, he'll either end up permanently knee-walking or his liver will eventually turn into a solid block of granite."

Brenda laughed as she backed the truck out and said, "You're not telling me anything I don't already know."

We waved goodbye as she pulled away. Tommy and I then did a shake of hands that turned into a bear hug. As we released our grip, I said, "Take it easy, buddy, and be real careful driving home."

"I certainly will," he said. "And you do the same. We surely do not need any more casualties around here."

I stood nearby as Tom got in his truck and drove off. I was about to get into my van when I heard the single strum of a guitar coming from inside the Blue Moon. Although I had already violated my standard practice of staying home on Saturday night, it had been for a good reason. I decided I just had to hear Luther play one more song, so I walked back inside and stood in the foyer.

Before starting to play, Lil' Luther announced, "We'd like to thank all of you good people for such a nice reception here tonight. It's been a real pleasure, and one I know we here in the band won't forget. We'd like to start out the last set of the evening with a B.B. King tune called 'You've Done Lost Your Good Thing Now.' We hope you'll enjoy it."

While Luther was speaking, he somehow picked out my face in the packed bar. He gave a slight nod of his head at the same time I made a small wave in his direction. I think we both knew this very well might be the last time we would ever see each other. Luther began the slow, emotional song with a guitar solo that couldn't have been played any more precisely by B.B. King himself.

The song spoke of the singer's love for his woman reversing itself with the lines, "Well the way I used to love you baby/Baby that's the way I hate you now." Yet he still made it clear that he longed to love her one more time. At that point in the song, I couldn't take it anymore and wandered back outside. The lyrics had gotten to me. The lines seemed so poignant to the fate of Wayne and Lisa that I just wanted to block everything out. Walking to my van, I couldn't help but hear the last part of the song coming out of the open windows on the side of the building. Luther sang the lyrics like he meant every word of it. He sang to his woman that she had earlier expressed her love, however, "Oh but the way you treat me now baby/I'd just soon rather be dead." Man, oh, man.

When the song was over, I got into my van and sat for a few minutes. My senses seemed deadened, more so from the overwhelming grievous experience than from the effects of drinking. Although, I'm sure that was contributing to my numb state of mind. I did a quick mental checklist of what had happened in one day's time. I had been to the funeral of a friend who had not made it to thirty years old. Also, there was a good chance I had lost my part-time girl friend. And I had probably seen an extremely talented musician put on an awe-inspiring show for the last time. Mentally and physically, I was exhausted.

I started the van and, with every remaining ounce of concentration, I drove carefully home. When I arrived, I parked the van in my driveway but I didn't feel like going inside. To go to bed and allow the day to be officially over would only seem to validate and solidify everything that had happened. Shoot, I thought, you can't make time stand still, can you? Still, I had this urge to want time to keep going in the present tense.

I grabbed a bottle of spring water out of the van and walked over to the beach. It was as clear and beautiful a night as the day had been. A light, warm breeze flowed over me as I stood near the edge of the water. Bright stars twinkled in the dark sky over the Gulf. As I took in the priceless splendor of the natural surroundings, I felt comforted. The allure of the outside world had a settling effect on my spirit, and I began to feel whole again. After fifteen or twenty minutes, I turned and left the beach. As I walked home, it struck me that the next day was Sunday and it meant a busy day at the cart. I was already looking forward to the regular group of seniors who walked on the beach. I couldn't wait to see them.

# 23

A month has passed since that night, and by following the standard, good advice of "stay busy" and "time heals," I have and it has, somewhat. There is still no adequate explanation for what happened to Wayne and Lisa, and there never will be. Working just to acquire possessions is no recipe for happiness. They were living, and are now deceased, examples of that. Happiness must come from within and, based on my experience last week with my parents, I have never been more certain of that.

For some months, my father had been battling lung cancer. The few times I'd talked with them, both of my parents had downplayed Dad's condition. I eventually learned he had gone through several procedures and had also been on a regular schedule of chemotherapy. Finally, my mother called and told me the end was very near. I flew up to my parents' house in Pennsylvania and, a few days after I arrived, Dad died. I stayed up north through the funeral and returned to St. George Beach last Sunday. When I got to my house, there was a message on my answering machine from Irving Rosenberg. He asked if I would give him a call when I got back home. He and Mildred knew where I had been and were aware my father had died. Since they kept an eye on my house while I was away, I had phoned them from up in Pennsylvania to let them know my stay was going to be extended so I could attend the funeral.

When I returned his call, Irv asked me if I would come over for our regular Sunday dinner together. He told me not to bother to bring anything but my appetite. At five o'clock, I walked down the street to their house. Irv greeted me at the door but, instead of our normal handshake, he put his arms around me and gave me a firm hug. It was the first time I could ever recall him doing that. He held onto me for a second and then said, "I'm very sorry about your father, Ellis."

"Thank you, Irv," I said. "At least he's not suffering anymore."

Mildred came out of the kitchen with tears in her eyes. She came over to me, arched her small frame up on her toes, hugged me, and said, "Oh, Ellis, I'm awfully sorry."

"Thanks, Mildred...thank you."

We all took a deep breath, and then Irv perked up and said, "How about a yellow bird cocktail to wet your whistle? You know, that's the one for luck."

"Sounds great," I said. "Perfect."

"And I whipped up a tray of appetizers, too," said Irv, giving me a little wink.

"Oh, Irving," said Mildred waving her hand, "you most certainly did not. Don't listen to him, Ellis."

We carried the trays of drinks and appetizers out to the lanai where Irv proposed a toast, "Here's to your father, Ellis."

We all said "Cheers" as we toasted our glasses. After nibbling in silence for a few minutes Irv said, "Ellis we're interested in how things went while you were up with your parents, but we don't want to pry. You talk about it only as much as you want to. You're the boss."

"Well," I said, "it was sad to see my father in such bad shape. He'd really been through a lot."

"So how's your mother doing?" said Irv.

"I guess at the end," I said, "she was almost kind of relieved the whole ordeal was over. She had been suffering right along with Dad. It will be tough for a while, but I think she'll be all right. My brother and his family live close by and they all have been very helpful. Mom also has a good support network of friends and neighbors who have pitched in, too."

"That's good to hear," said Mildred. "It's just such a shame."

"And how about you Ellis?" said Irv. "Are you going to be okay?"

"I'm glad you asked me that Irv," I said, "and the answer is yes. The day I got up to my parents' house, I sat with my father and we had a good talk. It was the deepest and most direct conversation I'd had with him since I moved down here sixteen years ago. As I've told you both many times, I haven't been very close to my parents since I came down here to live. I've felt like there had always been this under-current of disapproval on their part and, for a long time, I know there was. I think my own stubbornness had probably never made things any better, either. As we talked, my father finally addressed the subject. It helped us both open up to each other, and it was something that had been missing for a long time. He told me he had been wrong about not accepting what I had done with my life. Dad felt he had just wanted to help me be a success, but in reality it was only *his* concept of success. He told me there's no miracle blueprint for living. It's all individual. He said everyone has to live his or her life in their own way, and that's what makes it the most personal thing there is. He went on to say he was more certain of it all since he had been sick, than ever before. I thanked him and hugged him and we cried. We had made our peace at last."

I felt myself starting to lose it. I got up, excused myself, and went out the screened door of the lanai and walked to the edge of the canal. After a minute, I sensed Irv standing next to me. He reached up and put his hand on my shoulder. Looking straight ahead at the water, he said, "Life never ceases to amaze, Ellis. Just when you think you've got it figured out, it throws you a knuckleball. You've got to keep looking at it as work in progress. I'm glad you were able to have that talk with your father. I'm happy for you."

We then stood without speaking until a mullet in the canal directly in front of us broke the surface, flew airborne several feet, and then splashed flagrantly back into the water. It kind of startled us both back to a normal frame of mind.

"Come on," said Irv, "let's go in and eat dinner. Millie's got a seafood casserole in there that'll knock your socks off."

Irv was right. We had a delicious meal and mixed in good conversation. Although I pressed them on it, they both insisted there wasn't any list of household chores for me to help them with after we ate. Irv did point out, however, that I had better come prepared to work hard the following Sunday. He said he didn't want me to get in the habit of getting off too easy when it came to giving them a hand. You had to love the guy.

We said goodbye, and as I walked back up the street, I thought about how I cherished the times I spent with the Rosenbergs. Although they were old enough to be my grandparents, in essence they had been my surrogate parents for many years. I realized neither of them was going to live forever, but I decided not to spend too much time thinking about it. I would just enjoy them a week at a time and deal with the future when it arrived.

As I stepped onto my driveway and looked toward the garage, it struck me that the next day would be the start of a new week working at the cart. Since I had been away for a while, I needed to take an inventory of my provisions to see if I could make it until I got the delivery from my supplier on Friday. I decided to do it in the morning. I went around to the back patio, sat on the recliner, and checked out the canal until it got dark.

# Epilogue

So, things have sort of gotten back to normal around here. Almost everything except being with Marie on Wednesday nights, that is. By being away up north, I hadn't seen her for a few weeks. She called me the other day. I guess you could say she gave me 'the vegetable.' That's an old expression I remember from my short-lived stay in college. It's kind of a bland, and hopefully painless, way of saying things are over. She's been dating Mr. Right, or was it Dr. Martin, on a regular basis. Marie said things were going really well with them, and she thought it would be a bad idea for us to keep on with our previous arrangement. She's right. We both knew it had to end sometime. At some point, I'll have to pick up the couple of tank tops and pair of shorts that I had left at Marie's place. But if I don't ever get around to it, it'll be okay. The clothes are not a big deal.

Accepting the fact we are through will be tough for a while, but eventually I feel sure I'll get over it. Maybe it's something similar to when people say they don't fear death, they just fear dying. I'll still have my life here in paradise and I know I'll be happy about that. It's the transition period I'll have to work my way through. I still have feelings for Marie. I just think my feelings are different from what you'd consider traditional. I am glad for her, though. I hope she ends up happy, and if she does, she deserves it. Marie's a good person. I will miss her.

I've gotten back into the rest of my normal routine. Recently when I went down to fish off of the bridge over Gateway Pass, it felt kind of strange. It was the first time I'd been back there since Wayne's crash. I know I'm going to be all right, but the memory will take a long time to fade. I'm sure I'll never completely forget. The fact that I love the view from that bridge so much will help. It's my favorite. I don't know about Wayne, though. That's really a tough one to accept. He was a great guy. I'm going to miss him, too. Now I don't want to sound like a hard-ass or anything, but I don't think I'm going to miss Lisa very much. But then, I didn't have to deal with her very often. To get them both back, I'd trade the whole terrible tragedy for having things the way they were before. I mean, any time.

When I was up at the Blue Moon a few days ago, Tommy showed me a letter Lydia had received from Lil' Luther. It was postmarked from Memphis. Luther said things are going great. He's playing in a blues band with a regular gig at Mr. Handy's Blues Hall & Juke Joint. Years ago, W.C. Handy was considered one of the founding fathers of the blues. There's an awards ceremony every May in Memphis to honor his memory. It's sort of like the Grammys of the blues. Luther went on to say everything had worked out so well, his mother said it was okay for him to stay in Memphis. He's living with another guy who's in the band. It sounded like Luther was starting up the ladder to stardom. I hope everything works out for him. I'm going to keep my eyes and ears open for any word about him in music magazines and on the radio.

Tommy was pretty excited to hear the news too. Maybe one day Tommy and I will make a road trip up to Memphis and catch Luther's act in person. That'd be fun. At least now Tommy will have something to discuss with any customers who criticize the live music at the Blue Moon. For years, he'll be re-telling the story about the last night Luther played there, and what a wild time it was. Believe me, he will. And, no doubt, he'll be using his formal version of the English language. It seems there's also no doubt Tommy will remain an enduring fixture at the Blue Moon for a very long time. I can't see him ever doing anything else.

Then there's Harry. Yesterday he did his blocking-of-the-Boulevard maneuver with his flat-bed, right in front of my cart. He hollered at me to meet him over at the Shangri-La for a beer. He said there wasn't any crisis. He just wanted to talk and watch the babes on the beach, so I know he's back to his old self. When the drivers behind him started honking for him to move, he honked back and gave them the finger before he drove off. I could have pre-dicted he'd do that. Some people change and some people remain the same. Harry is one who will re-main the same. Harry is Harry and always will be. Someday, if we're old and gray in a nursing home, he will still be slapping backs, he will still be sling-ing the bull, and he will probably be telling the aides to "diaper this." What a guy. One of a kind. If I were pressed hard, I'd have to say I love him. But don't quote me on that. I don't want his head to get any bigger than it already is.

So I guess my life, in general, will go on pretty much like it has for years. In fact, business at my vendor cart should continue to improve with the increasing number of people moving to, and vacationing on, St. George Beach each year. If they want to keep buying the crap they call food from me, I'm not going to stand in their way. Being the wise businessman that I am, I will supply what they demand. I do know I don't want to expand my operation, though. I've got all I care to handle as it is and I'm happy about that. Come to think of it, I'm happy about most everything. I'm living where I want to live and doing what I want to do. And that's just fine with me.

Oh yeah, I almost forgot. There's this cute waitress who started working at the Beer Garden recently. She's from Costa Rica. I've talked to her the last couple of times I went there to eat. I'm unattached now, you know. She's got these dark eyes and a very pretty smile. Plus, she seems to have a head on her shoulders. If I get to know her a little bit better, I think I might ask her if she'd like to go out to dinner sometime.

# Acknowledgements

Thanks to Charles F. Woodring, III for technical assistance

Special thanks to Bob Sullivan for editorial assistance and valued advice